Miranda and Starlight

by

Janet Muirhead Hill

Book one of the Starlight Series

Followed by:

Starlight's Courage,
Starlight, Star Bright,
Starlight's Shooting Star
Starlight Shines for Miranda
and
Starlight Comes Home

(ordering information on the last page)

Thanks

to my friend and mentor, Florence Ore, for her consistent encouragement, positive criticism, willingness to read, read, and reread without flinching and for her faith in Miranda's story;

to my devoted husband, Stan Hill, and his unflagging belief in me, and

to my mother, Dorothy Muirhead, for her encouragement and support.

Miranda and Starlight

REVISED EDITION

Janet Muirhead Hill

Illustrated by

Pat Lehmkuhl

 Raven Publishing, Norris, Montana

Miranda and Starlight
Second Edition

by
Janet Muirhead Hill

Published by:
Raven Publishing
PO Box 2885
Norris, Montana
E-mail: Info@ravenpublishing.net

Text copyright 2003 © Janet Muirhead Hill
Illustrations copyright © 2003 Pat Lehmkuhl
Printed in the United States of America
ISBN: 0-9714161-4-1
Library of Congress Control Number: 2003093677

To Jayme Schaak

for asking,

"Grandma, will you tell me a story about a horse?"

The Horse

Here is nobility without conceit.
Friendship without envy. Beauty without vanity.
A willing servant, yet no slave.

Author Unknown

Chapter One

In the safety of the doorway of the fifth grade room, Miranda remained unnoticed. She cautiously observed the first day of school bedlam before daring to step in and become part of it. The teacher had arranged the desks into groups of four, two side by side, facing the other two. It made sort of a table with two people to a side. "Quad Pods," the teachers called them. Since their class was the smallest in the school with only eleven students, there were only three pods. Two were in the back half of the room near the bookshelves, and one was in the front, between the door and a circular table that had several chairs around it.

Miranda watched while her classmates claimed their territory in this new room. Two of the boys laughed over something hidden in a notebook, while two others headed to a group of desks in the back of the room.

Lisa and Kimberly, two of the five girls in her class, hurried to the remaining quad pod along the back wall. A girl Miranda had never seen before put her backpack on the desk across from Lisa. Miranda held her breath as she strained to listen to Lisa and Kimberly's reaction.

"Oh, that seat's saved!" Lisa exclaimed. "There are four of us. We always sit together."

"But I got here first," the new girl countered.

Miranda tensed, wondering how long this new girl would hold her own against the "Magnificent Four," as Miranda sarcastically called the only other girls in her class.

"So?" Kimberly asked loudly. "I just told you we need all four desks. There're three empty ones over there."

Miranda sighed as the new girl shrugged, picked up her backpack, and moved to the pod near the teacher's desk. She sat with her back to Miranda, across from a boy who was so engrossed in a book he didn't even look up.

Bet she feels as out of place as I did when I came here last spring, thought Miranda. *Those snooty girls don't like new kids coming to their school.*

"You gonna stand there all day?" demanded the familiar voice of Christopher Bergman, the class bully. "Either go in or get out of my way!"

A shove sent Miranda stumbling into the room. She slipped into the seat next to the new girl. The only place left for Christopher was across from Miranda.

She groaned and frowned at him as he sat down. Coming to school had been bad enough, but sitting across from Chris was almost more than she could take. In the two months Miranda had gone to Country View School before summer vacation, Chris had constantly teased and tormented her. That might not have been so bad if she had found other friends, but the other students were perfectly happy in their own little groups and no one wanted her to be part of them. Ignoring Miranda, but making sure she could hear them, Lisa and her friends often talked about their horses and their private riding club. They assumed Miranda was a city girl who didn't know how to ride.

If I just had a horse of my own, Miranda thought, *I'd show them!*

As the teacher passed out books to each student, Miranda stole a shy glance at the girl next to her. All she could see were the lovely curls that hung in waves to the desk top as the girl looked down at her own books. On a scrap of paper, Miranda scribbled, "Hi, I'm Miranda, what's your name?"

She slipped it past the curtain of dark brown hair and waited. Delicate fingers pulled the note out of sight but the new girl didn't turn to face her. Miranda sighed.

"This book," the teacher, Mrs. Penrose, was saying, holding a small book aloft, "will be our first reading book. We will read several novels throughout the year, and discuss them together."

Miranda picked up the book, "Julie of the

Wolves," from the pile on her desk. From the cover, an Eskimo girl stared straight at her, looking as alone as Miranda felt. Miranda opened the book. A nudge to her elbow sent the book flying to the floor. As she picked it up, she met the hard blue eyes of Mrs. Penrose. Miranda looked nervously at her teacher and tried to smile. When Mrs. Penrose looked away, Miranda turned to the new girl who pressed a note into her hand. Miranda spread the note open inside her book.

"I'm Laurie Langley. Do you want to come to my house after school?" the note said.

Miranda met her seat mate's soft brown eyes and smiled. A dimple flashed in Laurie's cheeks as she smiled back.

"Time for recess," called Mrs. Penrose. "Put your books away and line up behind Christopher at the door."

"Let's go to the office and use the phone," Miranda whispered, "I'll ask my grandma if I can go to your house."

When Miranda hung up the phone she faced the new girl with disappointment.

"I can't come today, Laurie. Grandma reminded me that Mom said she'd call tonight to see how my first day of school went. Mom thinks it's strange for school to start on a Wednesday," Miranda said as they reached the swings and claimed two empty ones.

"My mom said it's because Monday was Labor Day and the teachers needed Tuesday to get things ready. But where is your mother?" Laurie looked puzzled. "Did your grandma come to baby-sit while she's gone?"

Miranda drew a deep breath. *Here we go again*, she thought. She hated explaining her family situation to people.

"Mom's in California," Miranda began. "I'm living with my grandparents until she sends for me."

"That's a long way away! Has it been a long time since you've seen her?"

"It seems like it. I lived with her in Los Angeles for almost five years after we left here. She had a job with a modeling agency. She worked a lot and I had a nanny. But she got less and less work until she couldn't afford a nanny anymore, so she sent me back last March."

"Will she send for you soon?" Laurie asked in a troubled voice.

"I don't think so. Last I knew she had just moved in with some new roommates and was trying out for a part in a movie."

"Did you like living in Los Angeles?" Laurie asked.

"I liked my nanny," Miranda said. "But I missed Grandpa's farm. That's where I lived while Mom was going to modeling school. I don't care much for big cities, but I miss Mom."

"Do you want to go back and live with her?" Laurie asked.

"I don't know. I get all mixed up about it," Miranda said. "I'd rather she moved back here, but she loves the city. I think if Grandpa knew I'd be staying, he'd get another horse. He sold the one we had after I went to California."

"If a fairy suddenly came down and said you could have three wishes come true, what would they be?" Laurie asked.

"Well, ever since I came here last April, I've wished for a friend," Miranda said hopefully. "The other four girls in our class don't like me."

"I don't think they like me either," Laurie said. "But I'll be your friend. You're so much nicer than they are."

A warm feeling spread through Miranda's body and she couldn't help smiling.

"Hey, maybe there is a fairy. My first wish came true already," she said with a giggle.

"Make your second one. Maybe it'll come true, too," urged Laurie.

There was one wish that Miranda dreamed of night and day. She believed there was a chance it would come true, but was almost afraid to say it out loud for fear she'd jinx it. She decided to save it for last. Instead she told of one she wanted, but had no hope that she would ever get it.

"Well, I have one that even a fairy can't make come true. I wish I could have a real family with Mom and Dad and me all living together, close to Grandma and Grandpa."

"You told me about your mom, but what about your dad?" asked Laurie.

"I don't know. I've never seen him. I don't even have a picture to see what he looks like! All I know is that Mom says I look a lot like him. He left before I was born."

"You don't even know where he lives?"

"No. I don't even know if he's alive."

"That must be awful!" Laurie exclaimed. After a pause, she asked, "What is your third and final wish? Make it good 'cause I'm sure the fairy will grant you this one."

"More than anything in the world, I want a horse of my very own!" Miranda exclaimed quickly. "If I just had a horse, nothing else would matter."

"I like horses, too," said Laurie. "When we lived in Cincinnati, I took riding lessons."

"You lived in Cincinnati? Why did you move here?"

"After someone broke into our neighbor's house, Dad decided it was time to get out of the city. He wanted a safe place for me to grow up."

"Do you like it here?"

"I miss my friends but now that I have you, it won't be so bad," Laurie replied. "Have you had riding lessons?"

"My grandpa taught me to ride when I was little, almost before I could walk. He had a gray Quarter Horse that I rode everyday."

"My dad said he'd buy me a horse next summer," said Laurie. "You can ride it if you don't have yours yet. If you're still here, that is."

"I hope I have one, or I'll be the only girl in my class who doesn't," Miranda sighed.

Miranda tried to cover up the envy she heard in her own voice by giving her swing a big push and

shouting, "Someday I'm going to own a thousand horses!"

"Me, too." Laurie agreed. "I know! Maybe we could own a horse ranch together."

"Let's pretend we do," Miranda said. "Let's pretend we have the biggest horse ranch in Montana."

"Yeah, right!" bellowed a voice behind them. "While you two are dreaming, I'll be riding a real horse of my own."

"Christopher Bergman! How dare you sneak up behind us? Stop trying to scare people! It's not funny."

"I wasn't trying to scare you. You were just too busy wishing for horses to notice me," Chris said. "It's a good thing you don't have one, because you probably can't ride."

"Ha!" shouted Miranda. Her long ponytail swished against her cheek as she jumped off the swing and spun around to look into his freckled face. "I've ridden horses a lot more than you have. I don't believe you have a horse."

"Well, I do," Chris said. "My dad just bought me one."

"Yeah, sure. I suppose you keep it in your apartment," Miranda said, knowing Chris lived in town above the general store that his father owned.

"Haven't you ever heard of a stable?" Chris sneered. "We're boarding him at Shady Hills and I ride him every weekend."

"Yeah, right, Chris," Miranda sneered. "I bet

you don't know anything about horses."

"I do too! You're probably scared of horses. Look at you. You're so skinny, you have to stand twice to make a shadow!"

"At least I'm not so fat I'd break a horse's back. I hope your dad got you a work horse," said Miranda, who was rather proud of her slender body.

Christopher's eyes narrowed and his face turned red. For a moment, Miranda thought he was going to hit her.

"You're the one who doesn't know anything about horses," he shouted. "Your grandpa's nothing but a stupid dairy farmer who doesn't know a horse from a camel's butt. And your parents can't even take care of you, let alone buy you a horse."

Before she could stop herself, Miranda slammed her fist into his face.

"Yeoowww!" Chris screamed. "What did you do that for?"

His hand was bright red when he pulled it from his face. Blood streamed from his nose.

"Look what you did, Miranda!" Chris bellowed. "I'm going to tell Mrs. Evans!"

Miranda glanced at the teacher's assistant who was on recess duty. She was busy with some third grade boys who were fighting over the slide.

"Well, you shouldn't talk about my family like that," Miranda said, trying to hide her fear.

"Please, don't tell," Laurie pleaded for her new friend. "I'll get some tissues." She ran toward the schoolhouse.

"Does it hurt a lot?" asked Miranda, staring in astonishment at the blood on Chris's hands and face.

"You wish!" Chris yelled, blinking back tears. "You're not big enough to hurt me. Tell you what; I won't tell on you if you prove you're not scared of horses."

"How?" Miranda asked.

"By walking up to those two."

Miranda looked toward the field where Chris was pointing. Two horses were grazing near the school fence. Miranda forgot everything around her as she stared at the most beautiful horse she'd ever seen. A jet black stallion stood proudly, neck arched, as if standing guard over the lone mare grazing nearby. In her wildest dreams, Miranda had never imagined that such a creature could exist. She could tell he was young, probably no more than two and not quite full grown, but his features were delicate and finely chiseled.

Ignoring the "No Trespassing" sign, she climbed over the white board fence behind the cover of a tall cottonwood that stood in the corner of the playground and dropped into the field. Holding out her hand and talking softly, she approached the two horses. They pricked their ears forward and stared at her. Hesitantly, they walked forward. The pretty buckskin mare met her first, and Miranda patted her soft muzzle and stroked her neck.

"I dare you to get on!" shouted Chris who, with

Laurie, was watching from the fence.

Scratching the mare's back, Miranda ignored Chris, walked past the mare and extended her right hand toward the stallion. He eyed her curiously and let her touch his nose. Working her hand up to his cheek bone, she scratched him gently. He didn't move but watched her, his eyes alert and nostrils flaring. Continuing to stroke his neck, she slowly moved to his left side and stroked his withers. She murmured softly, "You're prettier than any horse I ever dreamed of. I'm going to make you mine someday. We're meant to be together; I just know it!"

"Hurry up, Miranda. What's the matter? You scared?" Chris prompted. "I knew it! You can't ride."

The young stallion stood still as a statue. Gripping his mane with both hands, Miranda jumped, pulled herself up and clapped her right leg across his back. The horse leaped into the air like an arrow shot from a bow, sprang sideways, and dashed away. Landing flat on her back, Miranda couldn't get her breath. She lay still, gasping. After running off a short distance, both horses circled back toward her as she rose shakily from the ground.

"Are you all right?" Laurie yelled, scrambling over the fence.

Miranda nodded and walked shakily toward her friend.

"See? I told you Miranda didn't know how to ride!" Chris exclaimed.

"I'd like to see you do any better!" Laurie shouted.

Miranda stopped and glared at Chris. She clenched her fist and bit her lip, to keep it from quivering. She couldn't let the bully think she was afraid.

"Just watch, Chris. I'll show you how to ride a horse!" Miranda declared, turning around.

The buckskin mare stood quietly in a small dip in the ground as Miranda approached her again. Talking softly and scratching her neck, she moved to the mare's left side. Grasping her mane, Miranda jumped as high as she could, and pulled herself up. In a moment, thanks to the mare's patience, Miranda straddled her. The mare still didn't move, as Miranda patted her neck and talked to her in soothing tones.

"Make it go!" shouted Christopher.

Nudging the horse with her knees, Miranda clucked softly. The mare started to walk and then to trot. Pressing her knee against the mare's right side, Miranda got her moving toward the school yard fence. The black horse had a different idea, however. Darting toward them, his head close to the ground and his ears back, he nipped at the buckskin's heels. The mare wheeled, burst into a gallop, and headed straight across the field toward a large barn. With a death hold on the short mane, Miranda pulled back with all her might. But the stallion kept up the chase, pushing the mare even faster. Miranda willed herself to stay on as she watched the ground blur beneath her. She heard the clanging of a bell behind her, marking the end of recess.

Chapter Two

"Whoa!" she yelled, pulling back on the handful of mane with all her strength.

Miranda had never ridden a horse this fast before. Her eyes watered and her mouth went dry. Looking ahead, she saw a pickup truck stop at the gate that divided the corrals from the field. A man jumped out and ran toward her, waving his arms. The stallion turned and galloped away, but the mare slowed to a bouncy trot that almost threw Miranda over her neck. She regained her balance as the mare stopped in front of the wild looking man.

"What the heck are you doing with my horse?" The man demanded as they came to a stop in front of him.

"I - I'm sorry," Miranda stammered as she slid off the horse.

"Sorry? What good is sorry now that the deed

is done?" The man's pale blue eyes glared beneath his shaggy gray eyebrows.

Miranda shook with fear, but she didn't look away.

"Don't just stand there. Answer me!" the horse owner snapped angrily. "Are you in the habit of helping yourself to other people's property?"

"No, sir," she said. "I didn't mean to actually ride her. I mean I wasn't planning on it."

"How do you get on a horse without planning on it? Don't lie to me or you'll make me downright mad. Who are you anyway?"

"Miranda Stevens."

"Stevens. I don't know anyone by the name of Stevens, and I know everyone in this county," the old man shouted. "Where do you live?"

"I live with my grandpa, John Greene, on his dairy."

"Oh, I know John Greene; sold him some hay for his milk cows a couple years ago. Well, he's going to be hearing from me. As for you, if you ever so much as set foot on my property or touch one of my horses again, I'll call the sheriff. Now skeedaddle!"

Miranda didn't have to be told twice. She ran across the field as fast as her legs would carry her. The schoolhouse was dwarfed in the distance and she had to slow down to catch her breath long before she got there, but she kept pushing on.

As she climbed over the fence, she didn't notice a nail sticking out of the top board. It snagged her shirt, ripping it all the way up the front as she jumped to the ground.

"Oh, no! What else can go wrong?" she asked herself as she trudged to the schoolhouse.

She took her jacket from a hook in the hallway and put it on to hide her torn shirt.

"Please be busy and don't notice me," she whispered as she opened the door cautiously and tiptoed into the classroom.

The room was quiet and the entire class looked up as she entered.

"Go to your desk, Miranda, and take out your math workbook. Do the problems on page eleven," directed Mrs. Penrose. "Back to work, everyone. No talking."

Miranda breathed a sigh of relief. Maybe she was going to get off easy. But when Mrs. Penrose told the students to line up for lunch, she asked Miranda to wait.

"Where were you after recess, Miranda?" she asked after the other students were gone.

"Well, I, uh," Miranda couldn't think of what to say.

"Just tell the truth, Miranda," said Mrs. Penrose. "It's a lot simpler and saves a whole lot of trouble in the long run."

Miranda took a deep breath and told her that "one of the kids" dared her to walk up to the horses and then get on one of them.

"I tried to make her stop, but she kept going

faster and faster until we were all the way across the field," Miranda continued.

She didn't mention Chris's bloodied nose, falling off the black stallion, or the angry horse owner. She added the part about ripping her shirt.

"It was very foolish to leave the school property and wrong to get on a horse that doesn't belong to you. You could've been hurt, or worse! I want a two page report from you, Miranda," Mrs. Penrose continued. "one page about why you should obey school rules, the other about respect for other people's property. You may start right now."

Miranda stared at her teacher, not wanting to believe she must miss recess. The teacher looked up again. "Now," she repeated.

Miranda sighed, sat down, and took a sheet of paper from her notebook.

"I hope you will learn a lesson from this," Mrs. Penrose said when Miranda turned her paper in. "I think your grandparents should know what you did. Do you want to tell them or should I?"

"I will," Miranda quickly replied. She hoped they weren't already hearing about it from the angry rancher. She didn't look forward to facing her grandparents.

As Miranda got off the bus, the front door flew open. Grandma appeared in the doorway, her hand shading her eyes from the afternoon sun.

She's looking for me, thought Miranda. *She must*

have heard from the grouch with the horses! She's going to kill me.

"Miranda. Miraaaanda," Grandma called. "Oh, there you are. Hurry. Your mother's waiting on the phone."

Miranda broke into a run.

"Is something wrong?" Miranda gasped as she reached the front porch.

"No," Grandma answered. "She called a little early because she has to go somewhere and won't be back until late."

"Hello," Miranda panted into the phone. As Grandma rolled out pie crust, Miranda studied her face. *She looks mad. I bet I'm going to catch it when I get off the phone*, she thought.

"What, Mom? Oh, fine! School's great. Guess what, Mom."

"I don't have much time to talk, Sweetie," Mom said. "I wanted to tell you something, though. I've been seeing this guy named Randy. He's real sweet and super handsome. He has a two-bedroom apartment and he's going to rent one bedroom to me real cheap. I'll move in next month. As soon as I get settled, you can come out and live with us. How does that sound?"

"What happened to John or Joe or whatever his name was?" Miranda frowned and took a piece of string from the cupboard drawer.

"You mean Jim. He turned out to be a jerk. You wouldn't have liked him, but you'll just love Randy. I can hardly wait for you to meet him. He's a singer in a nightclub. He has brown eyes, long, smoky blonde hair, a heavenly voice and. . . ."

Sick of hearing Mom rave about her various boyfriends, Miranda glanced around the big kitchen as she cradled the phone on her shoulder. Gleason, the fat tabby cat, was washing himself on the oval rug in front of the old-fashioned wood cook stove,

which they used only when the power went out.

"Miranda, are you listening?" asked Mom.

"Uh, yeah, Mom. Sounds nice."

"Oh, he is! Well, I'm almost late for an appointment. . . "

"I have a new friend at school," Miranda interrupted.

"That's nice," Mom said. "There's a school just a block from Randy's apartment. It's one of the biggest in the city. You'll be able to make a lot of friends when you come here. And guess what else; there's a big shopping mall . . . "

Miranda jumped down from the stool and swung the string in front of Gleason's nose. The cat tried to pounce on it as she pulled it away. Gleason turned a quick somersault and dashed under the kitchen table, peeking out from under the edge of the flowered tablecloth. The phone slipped from Miranda's shoulder and clattered to the floor. She scooped it up and hopped back onto the stool, capturing it between her chin and shoulder again.

"Oops! Sorry, Mom. I dropped the phone," she explained. "What were you saying?"

"I have to go, Baby. Someone's at the door." Mom sounded impatient. "I love you. Good-bye."

"But, Mom, wait! I wanted to tell you," Miranda began, but a click and dial tone told her Mom was no longer listening.

Miranda hung up the phone and headed for the bathroom.

"Supper will be ready soon," Grandma called after her. "Will you set the table please?"

"Just a minute, Grandma," Miranda answered.

Locking the bathroom door behind her, she leaned both elbows on the bathroom counter and stared at the freckled face in the mirror. Brooding gray-green eyes stared back at her. She watched them fill with tears as a knot of emotion rose from her chest into her throat. Frowning, she tried to sort out the rush of feelings that swelled inside her chest.

"You look madder than Grandpa's big bull," said the girl in the mirror, who was tugging at a long lock of hair the color of dirty sand.

"Well, anyone would be upset if her mother was a thousand miles away and only called to talk about her boyfriends!" Miranda replied indignantly.

She wrinkled her small, straight nose and twisted her delicate lips as she watched her reflection do the same. She couldn't remember when she had begun talking to herself in the mirror, but it had come to seem like a friend, separate from herself. When she needed to talk her feelings through, the girl in the mirror was someone she could trust to understand and keep secrets. Tears were washing over the freckles on the cheeks of the mirror-child.

"Are you mad or sad?" asked the reflection.

"Both," Miranda decided, "and scared, too. I really miss Mom, but I'm afraid to go to a new school where I don't know anyone. Even if I don't have a horse, I have a new friend. I have Grandma and

Grandpa. Why can't Mom come live with us?"

"They're never going to let you have a horse after getting in trouble for riding someone else's," warned the girl in the mirror.

Miranda sighed. "I wish Grandma and Grandpa could see that if I just had a horse of my own, I wouldn't keep getting into trouble. I don't really mean to, but you should have seen that horse. He's the most beautiful . . . "

"Miranda?" called Grandma from the kitchen.

"Coming, Grandma," she answered.

She put her thumbs in her ears and wiggled her fingers as she stuck out her tongue at the mirror. The mirror girl returned the compliment. Running cold water into her hands, she splashed some on her face, spilling some of it down the front of her jacket. Pulling it off, Miranda was surprised to see her torn shirt come off with it. She dashed to her room, tossed both jacket and shirt into the closet before pulling on a sweatshirt.

As she entered the kitchen, the back door slammed and Grandpa rushed in.

"Got a milk cow trying to calve! Looks like it's coming backward," he shouted. "I need both of you to come help." He was gone again, running toward the barn.

Miranda ran out the door with Grandma. She was surprised at how dark it had become and noticed that black clouds obscured the sun above the western horizon. The evening breeze had a cold bite to it. A big black and white cow was humped in a corner of the corral behind the barn. Around her neck was a rope, which Grandpa was wrapping around a fence post. The cow lay down, pulling the rope tight.

"Oops!" said Grandpa, quickly releasing it and wrapping it twice around the post nearer the ground. "Here, Miranda, hold the end of this rope and give her a little slack if she tries to stand up, but don't let her go."

Miranda took the rope and began to talk soothingly to the cow.

"Don't worry, old girl, Grandpa will help you. It hurts, doesn't it? Well, just relax and breathe, like this." Miranda huffed and puffed like women she'd seen in labor on TV shows.

Grandma and Grandpa were both holding onto a rope at the other end of the cow.

"Get ready. Now!" shouted Grandpa.

Together, they pulled the rope and fell backward when the calf slipped free. Grandpa scrambled to the still, wet mass on the ground. With his glove, he cleared away the membrane from the face of the calf and began blowing into its nostrils. In between breaths, he was thumping and massaging its body. Miranda stared, not realizing that she was holding her breath or that the cow was struggling to get to her feet.

"Miranda, let her stand," Grandma said softly.

"Oh," Miranda exclaimed. She let the rope slide around the post until the cow got to her feet.

"Hold her there," said Grandma.

Miranda saw that Grandpa still bent over the calf and knew that she must keep the cow from interfering. She had known of cows that would attack anyone who came near their babies. A moment later, she heard a gurgling little bellow and saw the calf move. Grandpa smiled.

"Now we can let Mama take over," he said as

he came to the cow's head and took the rope from Miranda. As soon as the rope was off the cow's neck, she hurried to her baby and began licking it.

With her grandparents, Miranda watched until the baby stood on wobbly legs and found the udder of warm milk. Tiny snowflakes were beginning to fall, and the wind roared in the trees across the meadow.

"Let's get them in the barn," Grandpa said, opening the door.

Miranda thought that would be hard to do, but Grandpa poured some grain into the manger and called, "C'm boss." The cow walked through the door as Grandma guided the calf behind her.

It was dark when they went back to the house, and Miranda shoved her hands into her pockets to try to get them warm.

Chapter Three

Miranda and her grandparents sat around the table in the kitchen. How warm and safe it felt. Miranda returned Grandpa's smile as he passed her a steaming plate of corn bread. She put a large piece on her plate and passed it on to Grandma. She sat dreamily, remembering the calf and, oh, the horses! Her stomach seemed to turn a flip as she remembered the trouble at school. She looked at Grandma, wondering if she had heard about it. Apparently Grandpa hadn't. When Grandma set a bowl of steaming stew on her plate, Miranda decided to tell them about the trouble with the horse owner, and get it over with. She took a deep breath, ready to begin.

"That was Belle, number 116," Grandma said as she picked up the record book she kept in the desk near the table. "It was a little bull, wasn't it?"

"Yep, a nice little fellow," Grandpa agreed. "Too

bad he got such a rough start, but I think he'll be okay now."

Miranda let out her breath slowly as she picked up her spoon. She tasted the warm stew and listened to the wind rattling the big window over the kitchen sink. Grandma and Grandpa talked about their herd of Holstein cows as Grandma referred to the book where names and dates as well as calving and milk records were neatly printed. Miranda's mind wandered to the horses she and Laurie would have on their dream ranch. They would have race horses and cow horses. Maybe they would even get a bunch of dude horses to take tourists on horseback rides through the mountain trails behind their ranch. They would have to name their horses and write them all down in their own record book. *Midnight,* she thought, *maybe that's what I'll name the black horse, or Shadow. If I had a buckskin like the one I rode . . .*

"Miranda, your grandpa asked how school was today," said Grandma.

"Oh, uh, sorry, I didn't hear you," Miranda stammered. "It was okay." She felt her face burn as she remembered the angry face of the horse owner.

"Anything the matter?" Grandpa asked, regarding her curiously.

"Uh, well," Miranda stirred her stew, trying to think how to tell them. She stalled by telling the good news first. "I have a new friend named Laurie. She's from Cincinnati. She asked me to come to her house after school. I couldn't today, because Mom was going to call. Could I go tomorrow?"

"Well, I don't know. I need to talk to her parents first," Grandma said.

Maybe if I tell them how it started, they'll see I need a horse of my own, Miranda thought. *If I tell them how beautiful they were, how it was a dare . . .* She took another deep breath.

"What did your mom have to say?" asked Grandpa, before Miranda could begin.

"Not much. She was in a hurry for a date or something."

Miranda took a bite of corn bread so she wouldn't have to talk about it. She would tell them about the trouble with the horses at bedtime.

"Miranda, I'll come tuck you in when I get back," Grandma said later, as Miranda was slipping into her pajamas. "Grandpa's going to help me cover the tomato plants. It's snowing, but if the plants are well covered, I don't think they'll freeze. They're loaded with green tomatoes and I'd sure like to see them ripen."

"Okay. Good night, Gram, 'night, Grandpa."

Miranda snuggled under her warm blankets and quickly fell asleep.

Laurie wasn't in school the next day. Recess was cold and bleak as the four-inch blanket of snow that had fallen overnight turned to slush. The wind blew in chilling gusts, and gray clouds scudded across the sky. It had been years since they'd seen such an early snowstorm, and the boys took full advantage of it. They made snow forts and hurled hard balls of snow at each other. The "Magnificent Four" giggled on the sidelines; cheering for certain boys and making fun of others. They screamed in pretended terror whenever a snowball shot in their direction. Miranda felt left out and lonely as she shuffled through the wet snow toward the swings.

Slam! A snowball hit her hard on the ear.

"Ow! Who did that?" she shouted, turning with tear-filled eyes toward the boys.

"What's the matter? Can't you take a joke?" asked Chris Bergman. "You aren't going to cry and run to the teacher, are you?"

"You jerk, Chris!" Miranda shouted as she ran toward him.

She molded a handful of snow into a hard ball of ice and flung it at Christopher. He ducked and it hit Bill Meredith in the neck.

"Jeez, Miranda!" Bill shouted. "You trying to kill me?"

"No, I'm trying to kill Chris," Miranda said. "Sorry, Bill, are you all right?"

Another snowball hit her in the mouth. She felt its sharp sting and tasted blood.

"Darn you, Chris!" she yelled.

She sprang forward and punched him in the back. He turned and shoved her backward into a puddle and ran.

"Oh no, you don't," Miranda yelled, diving at

his feet. He fell flat on his face.

"Miranda Stevens, stop that right now!" Mrs. Randolph, the kindergarten teacher, pulled her off Chris. "You apologize to Christopher and then go stand by the building until recess is over."

Miranda stomped off toward the building and leaned against it, arms folded over her chest. She glared at Christopher.

"Miranda," said Mrs. Randolph, "I didn't hear you apologize."

"I didn't."

"Miranda, tell Chris that you're sorry."

"I'm not sorry."

"You either apologize or go to the principal's office." Mrs. Randolph said as the bell rang.

"Sorry!" she snarled at Chris, making sure he understood she didn't mean it.

The knees and seat of Miranda's jeans were soaked from the slushy snow. She slid into her desk and sat shivering. Lisa leaned over Miranda's desk.

"The reason Chris picks on you is because he loves you," she whispered.

"Yeah, right," Miranda scoffed.

"He does! Don't you see how he looks at you?"

"No, because I never look at his ugly face. I hate him."

"Sure you do," Lisa said sarcastically.

"Lisa! Miranda!" Mrs. Penrose scolded. "Do you have something to share with the class?"

Both girls shook their heads, and Lisa hurried

to her desk.

At lunch, Chris plunked his tray onto the table and sat in the empty chair beside Miranda's. She turned her back and scooted away.

"Aw c'mon, Miranda," Chris said. "I'm not poison. I didn't mean for the snowball to hurt you. Can't you take a joke?"

Miranda moved farther away and went on eating without a word.

"Jeez, Miranda," Chris whined, "can't you accept an apology? You got me pretty good, you know. You're strong for a girl." Miranda picked up her tray and left the table.

By the afternoon recess, all the snow had gone from the school yard except for a white fringe next to the shady side of the building. Miranda crossed the playground, stood on the second rail of the fence, and rested her arms on the top one. She didn't dare climb over into the field for fear that Mrs. Penrose would find out. She hoped to coax the black stallion with the carrots in her pocket. But the field was empty. Not a horse of any size, shape, or color could be seen. *The grumpy old man must have locked them up so I couldn't get near them again,* Miranda thought. As she turned to go back to the school building, Chris stepped out of the shadow.

"How would you like to see my horse?" he asked.

"I don't care about your horse," Miranda lied.

"She's real pretty; tall and frisky. My dad

bought her from Cash Taylor."

Miranda guessed that was supposed to impress her, but she had no idea who Cash Taylor was.

"So?"

"She's a thoroughbred. I'm going to race her. She's a good jumper."

"What color is she?"

"Uh, sort of reddish brown," Chris stammered.

"Aha! You don't know. You don't even have a horse. You're making this whole thing up."

"I am not!" Chris declared. "I have a horse. She's a six-year-old, and I'm supposed to ride her three times a week."

Miranda noticed a change in Chris's voice, as if he were either angry or about to cry. "What's her name?" Miranda challenged.

"Queen of Royal Flush," Chris said. "I just call her Queen."

"If she were mine," Miranda said, "I'd ride her every day, not just three times a week."

"I haven't ridden her all that much," Chris admitted, looking at his hands as he twisted them together.

"Why in the world not?"

"Well, it's not like I don't have anything else to do!" he shouted.

"Don't get mad. I just don't get it. If I had a horse, I'd spend every spare minute riding with it."

"Well, I'm not you," Chris said.

"So, you really do have a horse?"

"I said I did, didn't I?"

"Maybe I would like to see her."

"I'm going over there tomorrow after school. If you want to come with me, I'll let you ride her."

"You're not lying to me, are you?" Miranda asked. "If I find out there is no horse, or if I don't get to ride, I'll never speak to you again!"

"Honest, Miranda. I wouldn't joke about this."

"Okay, Chris," Miranda agreed. "I'll ask Grandma if I can, but don't tell anyone."

"Don't want people to know you associate with me, huh?" Anger edged Chris's voice again. "Well don't worry."

Laurie was still absent from school on Friday, making it a very long day for Miranda. After school, she walked the quarter mile to the general store. From there, Chris's mother drove them across town and headed north on a gravel road. They turned left after a mile and soon came to a turnoff where a big sign, SHADY HILLS HORSE RANCH, arched over the entrance to a tree-lined lane on the left. For almost a mile down this winding corridor, Miranda saw no sign of any stables. When they crested a big hill, she looked down on the panoramic beauty of dazzling white fences and buildings among the trees. A framework of paddocks in the foreground extended from the side of a long white building.

"There're the stables!" Chris exclaimed, pointing. "That's Queen out in her paddock."

As they rounded another curve and rumbled across a cattle guard, Miranda saw a metal garage to her left. Beyond that, the gables of a tall white house were visible behind towering fir trees and the yellow-green leaves of aspen trees. Mrs. Bergman turned her mini-van into a lane between the stable row on the right, and a corral and some older buildings on the left. Beyond the large corral, Miranda saw a very familiar barn. A wave of panic seized her.

"Oh, no!" she murmured.

Chapter Four

As Mrs. Bergman stopped their new mini-van, Miranda stared at the white stable row, with two-part doors evenly spaced every few feet. A wooden sign engraved with a name hung above each door. Many of the top halves of the doors were open and soon filled with the heads of curious horses.

"They must think we're bringing them treats," laughed Miranda.

"Probably," agreed Mrs. Bergman, "but we're only allowed to feed our own. Mr. Taylor is very strict about that."

Miranda stepped cautiously from the mini-van, looking around for any sign of the old man who had yelled at her. Seeing no one, she started toward the row of stables to get a closer look at the horses.

"Thank you for coming to watch Christopher ride, Miranda. He's had riding lessons, and I think he'll impress you," Mrs. Bergman called to her. "I'm sure you'd like to ride, and we'd like to let you, but we just can't because of liability, you know. Please don't get too close to his horse; we don't want you getting hurt."

Miranda turned around in astonishment. She opened her mouth to say something, but closed it again and glared at Chris. He was closing the sliding side door of the van and apparently paying no attention to this new development.

Mrs. Bergman smiled at Chris and said, "You be careful, now," as she put the car in reverse and drove away.

With clinched fists Miranda strode toward Chris as the mini-van rumbled back across the cattle guard.

"Good grief, Chris," she yelled. "You're such a jerk!"

"What's the matter with you?" Chris asked as he walked past her to a sorrel mare that was nickering and bobbing her head up and down. "Come see Queen."

"She's beautiful!" For a moment Miranda forgot her anger at Chris, as she stroked the blazed face and soft pink muzzle. Queen's golden mane and forelock shone in the afternoon sun.

"Well, let's get to work," Christopher said.

"I didn't come here to work. I came to ride! And now I find out I'm not allowed to get near your horse, let alone ride her. Why the heck did you ask me to come, anyway?"

"You can ride. Mom and Dad will never know," Chris said matter-of-factly.

"There's something else you forgot to mention." Miranda snarled. "You could've told me this is where your horse is. I'm going to get in really big trouble if the owner finds me here!"

"I told you I kept her at Shady Hills. What do you mean, you didn't know?"

"Well, I never heard of Shady Hills before. I didn't know it was next to the school where I got in trouble for taking your stupid dare!"

"Jeez, Miranda! You must have your head in a bubble or something. I thought everyone knew where Shady Hills is."

"Well, I haven't lived here all my life, like you have," Miranda muttered, embarrassed that she hadn't paid more attention.

"So, Cash Taylor caught you riding his horse?" Chris seemed amused at the thought. "Last I saw, you were galloping away from school. I went in when the bell rang."

"Yeah, thanks a lot for your concern!" Miranda snarled. "Well, the horses took me straight to this tall guy with white hair and shaggy eyebrows. He had the meanest little eyes, and he yelled at me. He said if I ever set foot on his property again, he'll call the sheriff," Miranda said, shaking with fear and anger. "If he sees me, I'm dead! I shouldn't have trusted you."

"Come on in the tack shed," Chris whispered, reaching for her hand. "I'll see if he's around anywhere."

Miranda jerked her hand away but followed him through a door. The strong but pleasant smell of saddle leather and horse sweat caught her attention. She forgot Chris for a moment as she surveyed the well stocked tack room. In awe, she looked at the array of saddles on two rows of racks, one above the other, along two walls of the large room. Saddle pads and blankets were stacked in neat piles in one corner. Next to that, bins of brushes, curry combs, and hoof picks were under a shelf filled with bottles of fly spray, ointments, other medicines, tape, and bandages. Halters and bridles hung on hooks with a horse's name above each one. Ropes of many sizes and colors hung on more hooks.

"Coast clear; his car's not in the garage which means he's not here," Chris said, bursting through the door, beaming as if he had just done something stupendous. "Come on, you can ride first."

Miranda took the bridle Chris handed her and looked out cautiously before hurrying to Queen's stall. Chris followed, carrying a light English saddle.

"Where's the brush?" Miranda asked. "Grandpa said you're always supposed to brush a horse before you put the saddle on."

"Okay," Chris agreed, dropping the saddle. "I'll go get it."

As he hurried to the tack shed, Miranda studied the saddle. She didn't want to admit to Chris that she'd never ridden English. It couldn't be too hard.

"You can brush her if you want," Chris offered, handing Miranda the brush.

"Okay, but let's hurry. I don't want to get caught."

After giving the horse a quick once-over, Miranda struggled to get the saddle onto the tall mare's back.

"Is there anything we can stand on?"

"In the arena," Chris replied, leading the way.

As they passed the stable row on the way to the arena, Miranda peered into each stall. She was looking for her dream horse, the black stallion she had tried to ride on Chris's dare, but she didn't see him. Chris led her to a three-feet-high platform at the far end of the arena. From there it was easy to saddle the tall mare.

"I'll watch out the window for Mr. Taylor," Chris said as Miranda stepped into the stirrup.

Queen was gentle and obedient. Miranda started her at a walk, urged her into a trot, and then coaxed her into a gallop with just a little knee pressure and forward shift of her weight.

"She's a dream, Chris!" she said, finally bringing her to a stop near the boy. "You are so lucky!" She dropped to the ground and handed Chris the reins. "Thanks for letting me ride. Hope I didn't take too long a turn."

"Uh, no, that's okay," Chris said nervously.

"Miranda, there's something I have to tell you."

"What?"

"Well, I'm not real good at riding."

"That's okay. You haven't had her very long. I won't make fun of you."

"No, what I mean is, well, I thought, I mean I wondered if maybe you could help me."

"You want me to give you riding lessons?"

"Well, yes. Do you think you could?"

"I don't know. I would, except I can't keep coming here." Miranda thought of Mr. Taylor's angry threat. "But get on, and I'll watch you ride and give you some pointers."

"Well, all right," he said slowly. "Hold her still while I get on."

Miranda led Queen up close to the platform and held her still. She watched Chris approach the mare cautiously and clutch the saddle. He struggled to get his foot into the stirrup.

"Chris, not that leg. You'd be sitting on her backwards," Miranda said, giggling.

Chris turned red and backed away.

"Don't laugh at me, Miranda. Just because you can ride doesn't make you better than me!"

"I'm sorry. I didn't mean I'm better. It just looked so funny, the way you were trying to get on."

"Well, if you can't be nice, just stay away from me!" Chris yelled.

"Look, I'm sorry. Really," Miranda said. "I won't laugh and I won't tell anyone."

"Promise?"

"I promise!"

Chris stared at her for so long before speaking, that Miranda began to squirm.

"I haven't ever ridden her," he finally said.

"Are you serious?" Miranda asked in disbelief. "You told me that you rode three times a week."

"I did not! I said my dad or mom drops me off three times a week, but I don't ride. I just feed and water her. Then I chase her out of the stall so I can clean it without getting stepped on. When that's done I hang out until Mom comes to get me. It really gets boring."

"If you've had riding lessons, why can't you ride your horse?"

"It's a long story," Chris said dismally, "Last summer when my parents went on vacation to Europe, they sent me to a camp in Vermont. They signed me up to take riding lessons at camp. I went the first day and got this mean, ugly horse that bucked me off. I didn't want anyone to know I was scared, but I didn't want to ride either."

"So how did you make your parents believe you did?"

"Well, there was this kid in my cabin who really wanted to ride, but he hadn't gotten into the class, because, even though there were lots of horses and several teachers, it was full before he got there. So, he and I switched names. I was Dale Johnson for a whole month. It was kind of fun. I got certificates in entomology and geology and he got one in horsemanship. They even had a show and he won two blue ribbons. They're hanging on my bedroom wall. How was I supposed to know Dad would decide to surprise me with a horse?"

"Jeez, Chris!"

"Miranda, please don't tell anyone," Chris begged. "And please help me ride so I don't have to tell my dad. He signed me up to ride in a horse show at the Bozeman Winter Fair in January, so I have to learn to ride by then."

"But I'll get into big trouble if I keep coming here."

"Please. I can't tell those other snooty girls in our class, and I don't want the guys to know I'm scared of horses! I can't ask any of the grownups around here; they'd tell my dad." Chris was actually on his knees. "I'll keep watch so Mr. Taylor won't see you."

"Well, all right, I'll try it for awhile," Miranda agreed. "But if I get in trouble, you're toast!"

She began by showing Chris how to get on and off. From the platform, it was easy to reach the stirrups and Queen stood patiently still. Next, Miranda explained two kinds of reining; neck reining and what her grandfather called plow reining.

"I think that's how they do it with English riding, but I'm not sure," Miranda admitted.

She explained about knee pressure, and showed how quickly Queen responded to it.

"Whoever trained this horse sure knew what they were doing," she said as she dismounted. "Now, you try it."

"Next time, Miranda," he said. "She looks a little frisky."

"I just rode her, Chris. Sure, she has some life, but she's easy to control."

"We'd better clean the stall," Chris said. "It hasn't been done for two days. Mr. Taylor will hit the roof if he sees it."

"I thought you wanted me to teach you."

"I do, but, I already learned some things and I can ride next time. I really am worried about Mr. Taylor seeing her stall."

"Well, I didn't come here to do your dirty work for you," Miranda said. "You clean the stall. I'll work your horse. Where can I ride outside?"

"There's a gate at the end of the paddock into the river pasture. Mr. Taylor said I could ride there. He said there are lots of trails."

"Great! I'll be back by the time you're done."

"Don't be late," Chris warned, "Mom'll be here in half an hour. She'd better not see you riding."

In the sheer joy of riding along the river, Miranda forgot everything else. When she finally looked at her watch, twenty minutes had passed. She turned the mare and let her run, even though she knew that running to the barn was poor horse training. She got off at the paddock gate and led Queen the rest of the way to the back stable door. She stopped when she heard voices in Queen's stall. Holding her breath, Miranda flattened herself against the side of the stable and peeked around the door frame. There, towering over Chris, was Mr. Cash Taylor.

Chapter Five

"If your stall ever gets as dirty as I saw it this afternoon, I'll charge you a penalty!" Mr. Taylor shouted. "It isn't healthy for the horse and it makes me look bad."

Miranda climbed over the fence and slipped into the stall next to Queen's.

"Don't make me sorry I sold my prize mare to your father." Miranda held her breath as Mr. Taylor's voice rose to a scream. "What the Devil? You haven't unsaddled her yet and she's sweating! I don't care what else you have to do, never leave a hot horse standing in the cold. Now get out there and walk her until she's cool, then clean her up before you turn her loose." He walked away, still lecturing, "Your parents said you were such an expert horseman. I'd better start seeing some evidence of it if you're going to keep that mare on my property!"

As soon as he disappeared, Chris hissed, "Miranda, where are you?"

"Here," she said, clambering back over the fence. "I'm sorry. I usually don't run a horse back to the barn, but I was afraid your mom would get here before I did."

Even as she spoke, Mrs. Bergman's mini-van stopped in front of the stable. Miranda quickly unfastened the billet straps and pulled the saddle and pad off the mare.

"Lead her around to cool her down, Chris. I'll tell your mom I'm putting the saddle away for you. She didn't say I couldn't do that."

Chris nervously picked up the reins and started down the paddock, looking over his shoulder to make sure Queen didn't step on his heels.

"Walk beside her so you don't get stepped on, Chris!" Miranda yelled.

Turning, she almost bumped into Chris's mother. "Oh, hi, Mrs. Bergman. Chris is walking Queen to cool her off. I'm just putting his saddle away for him."

"Oh, dear, he shouldn't make you do the heavy work. Did he make you clean the stall, too?"

"No, Chris did that, but I don't mind helping. This saddle isn't nearly as heavy as my grandpa's western saddle," Miranda answered.

"Is Chris about ready to go?" Mrs. Bergman asked. "I have a bridge party to get ready for."

"He still has to brush her. Could I help do that?"

Miranda asked. "I've worked with horses before."

"I can't have you getting stepped on," Mrs. Bergman replied.

"I promise I won't. It would help him finish faster."

"Oh, all right," Mrs. Bergman sighed. "But be careful! I'll wait for you in the car."

Miranda snatched the halter off the peg by the door and ran to meet Chris. She slipped off the bridle and put the halter on. Together they brushed her coat to a copper sheen, Chris concentrating on the neck and shoulders while Miranda groomed the rest of the horse, including each leg. She picked the soil out of each hoof.

"How come you aren't afraid to do that?" Chris asked.

"How come you are?" Miranda asked in turn. "It's all part of taking care of a horse. It's fun if you love horses like I do."

"Well, hurry up. Mom's honking the horn. Let's get out of here before Cash Taylor sees you," Chris said.

With a last caress, Miranda slipped off the halter and handed it to Chris.

"Put this away while I give her some grain and hay," Miranda instructed, "and run a little more water in her trough."

She and Chris jumped into the mini-van just as Mr. Taylor emerged from the garage and headed to the house. Miranda ducked behind the seat as the car sped past him. When the car climbed the first hill, Miranda ventured a backward look. A thrill passed through her as she glimpsed the young black stallion in one of the paddocks.

"Are you going to ride tomorrow?" Miranda asked Chris as Mrs. Bergman pulled into her driveway.

"No, we have to go visit my grandparents in Billings. We'll be gone all weekend."

"Oh." Miranda was disappointed. "Well, see you Monday."

Laurie met Miranda on the playground Monday morning, smiling eagerly.

"Miranda, I've been waiting for you. I had the flu and had to stay home Thursday and Friday. It was really boring; I'd rather be in school."

"I missed you, too, especially over the weekend," Miranda said.

"Do you think you could come to my house after school?"

"Well, uh," Miranda stammered, "I'd like to but. . ."

"But what?" Laurie demanded.

"Well, I sort of had other plans."

"What plans?" Laurie frowned. After a second thought, she added. "You don't have to tell me if you don't want to."

Miranda didn't want to hurt her new friend's feelings, so she whispered, "I'm going to ride Chris

Bergman's horse, but don't tell anyone."

Laurie's mouth dropped open. "Does he really have a horse? He'd let you ride it?"

"Yes! He's having me give him some pointers, but I wasn't supposed to tell anyone."

"Please let me go, too." Laurie begged. "I'd like to ride."

"I don't know about riding. Mrs. Bergman doesn't really want us to, so don't tell her. First, we'll have to ask Chris, and he'll be mad that I told you."

Miranda was right; Chris was angry!

"Why did you tell her, Miranda?"

"She's my best friend. We don't keep secrets from each other. I won't tell anyone else, I promise," Miranda said.

"Like I can trust you," growled Chris. "Well she can't go! Before you know it, the whole school will be laughing at me."

"For what, Chris? That you have a horse?" Laurie asked. "Miranda just said she's giving you some pointers. Is that what you're ashamed of?"

"Oh," said Chris. "Well, be at the store with Miranda, but I don't know what my mother will say."

An hour and a half later, they found out why Chris was worried about his mother's reaction. Miranda waited for Chris to introduce Laurie to her. When he didn't, she said, "Mrs. Bergman, this is my best friend, Laurie. Chris said she could go with us so she can see his horse, too."

"What? Well, I don't think that's a good idea.

One at a time would be better. I'm not sure how Mr. Taylor will feel about having extra kids at his stables," Mrs. Bergman said.

"Oh, Mrs. Bergman. I'll be so still and quiet no one will know I'm there,"

"Well, I guess, since you're here," Mrs. Bergman said, "But if I get any complaints from Mr. Taylor, it will be the last time I take either of you girls back to Shady Hills."

As they drove down the road toward Shady Hills, they met a big black Cadillac heading in the opposite direction. "That's Mr. Taylor," said Chris, with a meaningful glance at Miranda as she shrunk back into the seat.

Miranda had Chris do more of the work, showing him how to put on the bridle, pad, and saddle. He was scared at first to reach under her girth for the billet, but did it anyway when she laughed at his fear.

"She's as gentle as a kitten, Chris!" Miranda explained. "She won't hurt you."

He still insisted that Miranda ride first. She rode in a figure-eight pattern as she showed him how to hold the reins, how to apply leg pressure, and what voice signals Queen obeyed. Finally, after Miranda insisted he try it, he agreed to get on.

"If you tell anyone I'm just learning to ride, Laurie, I won't let you come back here," Chris warned. "You'd better not laugh at me either!"

"I won't, Chris." Laurie assured him. "Don't

be embarrassed. I was scared when I started riding, too."

Miranda led the horse at first because Chris was literally shaking with fright.

"Calm down, Chris," she said, "You're making Queen nervous. Just relax and hold on. I'll hold on to her for awhile."

After a slow walk around the arena, Chris had gained a little confidence. Continuing to walk beside him after Chris took the reins, Miranda lectured him about the right amount of pressure to use.

"Don't pull back so hard, Chris. She doesn't

need it and it hurts her mouth."

When they returned to the stable, Chris let Laurie ride up and down the paddock while he cleaned the stall. Miranda hurried down the row of stables peering into each stall. At last she found what she was looking for.

"Wow! Here you are!" she exclaimed to the black colt. "Remember me, you beautiful boy? You and I are going to be friends."

She patted his velvety black nose and rubbed his arched neck. As he lowered his head, she swept the coal black forelock from his face, revealing a perfect four pointed white star in the middle of his forehead. She looked at the name above his door.

"Sir Jet Propelled Cadillac," Miranda read. "What an ugly name for the prettiest animal on earth. No, that will never do!"

She opened the door and stepped inside, looking him over from his perfect head and arched neck to his long, delicate legs and small black hooves. Not a spot of white could she find on him, except for the star on his brow. She walked around him, petting him softly and murmuring, "Oh, you pretty boy. I'd give anything in the world to have you for my own. I'd call you Starlight and treat you like a king."

The black colt began to move toward the open back door into his paddock.

"Wait," Miranda said, circling her arm around his neck.

But the horse pushed past her so suddenly she

almost fell down. She watched as he put his head down, kicked up his heels, and broke into a full gallop, head high and black tail furled like a flag. Quickly covering the length of the paddock, he skidded to a stop at the barred gate.

Miranda, dazzled by the wild beauty of his flight, ran after him. When she drew near she slowed to a walk and held out her hand, trying to coax him to come to her. He looked up once and began cropping the short grass as if he were no longer interested in her.

Talking softly, Miranda approached slowly. He kept on grazing as she stroked his neck. Keeping her hand in contact with his body, she walked behind him and to his head. He seemed unconcerned. She scratched between his ears again, and he raised his head to look at her.

"What are you doing here?" A booming voice in the distance startled her. She looked up to see Laurie sitting on the fence watching Chris unsaddle Queen in her paddock. At first she couldn't see where the unmistakable voice had come from. Then Mr. Taylor emerged from Queen's stall into the sunlight.

Miranda dropped to the ground and looked for a place to hide. Sliding back the bar, she opened the gate just enough to slip through and closed it quickly. Holding the gate closed, she crouched behind it.

She couldn't hear Laurie's reply. Then Chris said something she couldn't understand either.

"Well, stay out of the way and don't bother the

other horses," Mr. Taylor shouted.

Miranda lay low until she heard a car door slam and the an engine roar to life. She stood up cautiously and peered toward the road where it ran parallel to the paddocks. She heard the rumble of the cattle guard before she could see a cloud of dust rising behind a black car. Breathing easier, she slipped back through the gate.

Starlight grazed close to the rail fence. Miranda patted him as she slid between him and the fence. He paid little attention to her as he reached with his nose beneath the bottom rail to nibble the grass. Slowly climbing up the fence that pressed against her back, Miranda continued stroking Starlight. When she stood on the second rail from the top, she could easily reach her leg across his back and lower herself to straddle him. Her heart pounded as she did so.

Starlight jerked his head up and reared. Gripping his mane with both hands, Miranda crouched low over his neck and withers and tightened her legs against his sides. He backed into the gate and it swung wide open. She'd forgotten to latch it. Sensing his freedom, Starlight wheeled and dashed down the lane into the pasture. Miranda clung to his mane as fences and trees flew past in a blur. She could feel the power of muscles surging against her legs, filling her with both fear and awe. Starlight left the bridle path and dashed into the woods. Miranda saw a small stream coming up fast and prepared for a flying leap. Instead, Starlight jolted to a stop. Miranda didn't. She sailed in an arc over his head and landed on her back on the other side of the stream.

The breath was knocked out of her, and she lay gasping, filled with panic at not being able to breathe. When she could finally fill her lungs again, she rolled onto her knees and looked for Starlight. She saw him disappear into a thicket of willows. Jumping from stone to stone, she crossed the shallow stream and ran after him.

In the willows, the ground was wet and marshy. Hearing a frightened neigh, she rushed on. She stopped in her tracks when she saw him. Kicking wildly, he bucked and spun in a circle until he fell to the ground where he continued to thrash and squeal. A rim of white showed around his terror filled eyes.

"Whoa, boy, whoa!" Miranda yelled. "Why are you acting so crazy?"

Something snapped against her leg, nearly knocking her down. She reached down to see a rusty strand of barbed-wire hooked in her pant's leg. An old fence that had once stretched across the bog lay looped and tangled from one rotting fence post to a coil that was nearly buried near the edge of the swamp. Starlight reared and plunged, but each twist and lunge only tightened the wire around his back leg. One more spin and the wire stretched around his chest. He fell face first into the mud and struggled up again, kicking and squealing. The more he struggled, the more it tightened around him until it pulled him down again.

"Oh, please stop, Starlight!" Miranda screamed.

But he didn't quit struggling until he spent himself in exhaustion. When Miranda reached out to calm him, he began fighting again until she backed away.

Chapter Six

As Miranda climbed over the gate into Queen's paddock, she yelled, "Chris! Laurie!" but they didn't hear her.

She plunged on, half stumbling to the back door of Queen's stall.

"Miranda! Where have you been?" asked Chris.

"Are you all right?" asked Laurie, hurrying to where Miranda bent over, hands on knees, gasping for breath.

"Go get Mr. Taylor! Hurry! Starlight," Miranda had to catch her breath before she could go on.

"Mr. Taylor left," Chris informed her.

"We have to tell someone. He's tangled in some barbed wire and he can't get loose!"

"Who is?"

"Starlight. . . a horse. One of Mr. Taylor's

horses. We've got to hurry."

"We can't! Here comes Mom," Chris said. "If we keep her waiting she won't let you come again!"

"I've got to get help!" Miranda tried to make Chris understand.

"There's Higgins. Tell him. But hurry!"

Miranda ran toward the hay barn where an old man was loading some bales onto a pickup.

"Please, you've got to help Starlight," Miranda gasped.

"Who?"

"There's a horse in the pasture. He's all tangled up in barbed-wire. He's lying in the mud and he can't get up."

The old man cursed under his breath.

"I knew that wire would get us in trouble before we got someone to pick it up! I'll get some help and get right down there."

"I can show you where he is," Miranda offered, ready to run.

"No need. I know where the wire was left. The ranch hand who quit last week said he wasn't going to go wallowing through the bog to pick it up."

Miranda heard the impatient blast of a horn and saw Mrs. Bergman's van driving toward her.

"You'd better go," the old man said. "Don't worry, I'll take care of it."

"Grandma," said Miranda nervously as she set the table, "I want to go for a walk after dinner."

"A walk?" asked Grandma. "You and me?"

"No, by myself."

Miranda figured she could walk the mile and a half to school in a half-hour if she hurried and by crossing the field she could get to Shady Hills the back way. She just had to know if Starlight was all right. If they hadn't rescued him yet, maybe she could help.

"Since when have you taken up walking?" Grandma asked. "It'll soon be dark."

"I'd like to get some exercise before I go to bed," Miranda said.

"But you just got home from helping Chris with his horse," Grandma looked puzzled. "What about homework?"

"I don't have any."

"Don't you have spelling words to study?" Grandma asked. "And I think you're behind on your reading."

"If I finish before bedtime, may I go?" Miranda asked.

"It'll be dark by then," Grandma answered. "Right now, let's get these dishes done."

"Ooouh!" Miranda groaned. "Do I have to?"

"Yes, you always do. Is there something you'd like to talk about?"

"No," Miranda said with a frown as she stomped across the kitchen with her dishes.

"Miranda, you're acting very strangely, to-night," Grandma said. "What's going on?"

Miranda looked down, suddenly ashamed of

the way she was acting.

"Sorry, Gram. I'm worried about one of Mr. Taylor's horses. Just before I left today, he got caught in some barbed-wire. I want to see if he's okay."

"Why didn't you say so? We can call Mr. Taylor and ask him."

"No. I don't think it's a good idea to bother him."

"Why not? He knows about it, doesn't he?"

"I think so. He wasn't home when it happened but a man who works for him was taking care of it."

"Then don't worry about it. There's nothing you could do. You'd just be in the way. You can ask about it tomorrow."

Miranda sighed. Grandma was probably right. Besides, if Miranda pushed the issue, Grandma might actually call. Then she'd find out that Mr. Taylor had forbidden her to be there. He might even sue her grandparents if he figured out that it was her fault.

When the dishes and her studies were finally done, she locked herself in the bathroom and stared into the mirror.

"I've really gotten myself into a lot of trouble!" she said to her mirror friend.

"Yeah. Taylor's sure to find out it was you who let his horse out. The old man will tell him."

Tears streamed down the mirror-child's face as Miranda sobbed. "That means I'll never be allowed to see Starlight again. Oh, what have I done?"

When Miranda went out to feed the chickens and her bunnies the next morning, she was surprised to see a three-inch blanket of snow covering everything. It transformed the world into a fairy land that filled her with energy and made her forget Starlight for a few moments. She loved the snow and liked feeding her pets.

By the time she came back to the house for breakfast, however, a knot in the pit of her stomach made it impossible to eat. All she could think of was

how frightened and helpless Starlight had looked when she left him. Tears stung her eyes when she remembered the wild ride through the pasture. She'd felt the power of his muscles beneath her, and now she feared he'd never run like that again.

At school, the day dragged on and on for Miranda. She stared out the window, worrying about Starlight and wondering how she could see him without getting into further trouble with the owner. At recess Laurie wanted to play horse ranch, but Miranda's heart wasn't in it.

"What's wrong, Miranda?" Laurie asked.

"You know the horse that was tangled in barbed-wire? Well, it was my fault! I was just going to try sitting on him, but the gate wasn't shut tight and he got out of his paddock." Miranda confessed, hanging her head. "I love him and I can't think of anything else until I know he's all right. I'm going over there with Chris as soon as school's out."

"You got on him?" Laurie asked in amazement.

She wanted to know everything, so Miranda told her, as they sat on the swings, their heads close together, their voices low.

"No wonder you're upset. It's a wonder you weren't killed. I don't know how you get the nerve to get on horses that aren't even tamed yet." Laurie said.

Miranda shrugged, unable to explain the urge that prompted her to mount him.

"May I go with you to Shady Hills?" Laurie asked.

"Sure, I want you to come. Let's go ask Chris."

They found him alone under the slide, stock-piling snowballs.

"I'm not going to ride today," Chris answered.

"Why not?" Laurie asked.

"Yeah, why not?" Miranda echoed.

"It snowed, in case you haven't noticed," Chris sneered.

"So what? They have an indoor arena if you're afraid of riding in a little snow," said Miranda. "Besides, it's melting."

"Look, I don't have to ride Queen everyday just because you want to."

"But what about feeding her and cleaning the stall?" challenged Miranda. "That has to be done everyday."

"Dad pays Higgins to do it. All I have to do is call him and say I won't be there."

"Who's Higgins," asked Miranda.

"The old guy you talked to yesterday. He works for Mr. Taylor," Chris explained with a wave of his hand. "I forgot to call the last two days I wasn't there, so he didn't do it, and I'm the one who gets in trouble," Chris complained. "You'd think he'd notice I wasn't there."

"You have it so easy, Chris!" Miranda said angrily, "And you don't even appreciate it."

"Come to my house, then," Laurie said to Miranda. "You haven't been over yet."

Miranda sighed. "I'll call Grandma and ask. I'm

sure she'll let me because she thought I'd be going with Chris."

"You better not have told her you're riding my horse, because if she tells my mom we're both in trouble," Chris growled.

"Duh! I'm not stupid, Chris!" Miranda replied as she walked away. Sometimes she wondered how she could stand to be around him.

"By the way, Miranda," Chris said, following the two girls, "I'm not going to the stables tomorrow either. I have an appointment to get my eyes checked after school."

"Fine!" Miranda whirled around. "You don't want to learn to ride, do you? Too bad that such a beautiful horse belongs to a lazy dork like you!"

Miranda stomped away, overwhelmed by sudden anger.

"You think you know everything!" Chris called after her. "Well, you're not half as smart as you think you are!"

"Stop following us around or I'll punch you in the face again!" Miranda shouted.

She was startled to see a look of fear and pain in Chris's eyes before he bolted away from her when the bell signaled the end of recess.

"Last one to line up is a rotten egg!" he shouted.

"Jerk," Miranda muttered as she and Laurie trudged toward the building.

The sun was shining when Miranda and Laurie

left school that afternoon. They shuffled through the slush to Laurie's house.

"Let's forget about Chris and have a good time," said Laurie. "I've been wanting you to come to my house ever since the first day we met. I'll show you my horse collection and . . ."

Laurie chattered on as they walked down the sidewalk, but Miranda's thoughts turned to Starlight. She had to think of a way to get Mr. Taylor to sell him to her. Higgins said they were short handed. Maybe she could work for them. If she could make Mr. Taylor listen, she'd confess everything. Then she'd demand that he give her a chance. It was her fault that Starlight got hurt, so he should leave her grandparents out of it. That's what she'd tell Cash Taylor! She could clean stables, groom horses, and feed.

"Miranda! Are you listening?" Laurie was tapping her shoulder. "I asked what you want to do."

"Oh, whatever you want to do," Miranda said. "What do you have to play with?"

"You didn't hear a word I said, did you?" Laurie accused. "What were you thinking about?"

"Oh, Laurie, I'm so worried about Starlight, I can hardly stand it."

"Oh, yeah. You must feel terrible, but what can you do?"

"I don't know," Miranda replied miserably.

Laurie opened a gate in a white picket fence that surrounded a big yard.

"Here's where I live," she said.

The yard was as neat as the old style two story brick house at the end of the flagstone walk. Shrubbery and beds of flowers, bedraggled by the heavy snow, nestled against the house. Melting snow dripped from broad leaves of the tall poplars, cottonwood, and aspen trees that surrounded the house on three sides.

"What a pretty place!" Miranda exclaimed.

Laurie smiled. She held the door for Miranda and led her through a huge living room and past a stone fireplace that opened into both the living room and dining room.

"Come into the kitchen," Laurie invited.

Miranda walked through the dining room where large white-framed windows displayed the afternoon sun and a beautiful view of the back garden. Laurie led the way through swinging doors.

"Mom has a snack for us," Laurie said. "Mom, this is my best friend, Miranda."

Mrs. Langley's blue eyes sparkled as she held out her slender hand and smiled brightly. "What a pleasant surprise, Miranda. I'm glad you could come so I can finally meet this wonder-girl that Laurie is always talking about."

"What have you said about me, Laurie?" Miranda asked, as she returned Mrs. Langley's infectious smile.

"Just the truth," Laurie smiled.

After nibbling on apple slices dipped in cherry-flavored cream cheese and sipping hot cider, the girls climbed the stairs to Laurie's room. Miranda admired the beautiful dolls that filled the shelf above Laurie's bed, but was even more fascinated with the horse models that stood on her bookcases and chest of drawers. Miranda picked up a rearing black stallion that reminded her of Starlight.

"Do you want to play Monopoly, Rumicube, or cards?" Laurie asked as she opened her closet.

"Laurie, you're wanted on the phone," called Mrs. Langley before Miranda could answer. "It's Mrs. Bergman."

"What in the world could she want?" Laurie asked Miranda as she ran into the hallway and picked up the phone.

"Got it, Mom," she shouted down the stairs. "Hello?"

"But, Mrs. Bergman, I didn't do it!" Miranda heard her friend say. "I never went near any horse but Queen. I didn't opened any gates!"

Miranda could hear Mrs. Bergman's voice crackling loudly, but couldn't make out the words.

"Fine, but I didn't do anything wrong!" Laurie protested and hung up.

"They think you opened Starlight's gate, don't they?" asked Miranda as Laurie hung up.

Laurie nodded and Miranda saw a tear glisten in the corner of Laurie's eye.

"But why? I told Higgins where he was. Why would they think it was you?"

"I don't know, but they do. Maybe Mrs.

Bergman just doesn't like me. Or Mr. Taylor; he was sure mad that I was there, so maybe he accused me," Laurie said, with tears in her eyes. "All I know is that Mrs. Bergman told me Mr. Taylor called and said never bring that curly, brown-haired girl to Shady Hills Ranch again."

"Oh, Laurie, I'm sorry." Miranda said, putting an arm around her friend's shoulders. "Is Starlight hurt very bad?"

"Mr. Taylor says he's ruined and that he'll have to sell him for dog food."

Miranda was stunned. She could neither move nor speak as hot tears trickled down her cheeks.

Chapter Seven

Miranda couldn't sleep. After Grandma and Grandpa were in bed, she dressed and went outdoors. Struck by a cold wet wind, she went back for her cap and mittens.

"Miranda?" called Grandma as Miranda tiptoed past her grandparents' bedroom.

Miranda held her breath and didn't answer.

"Miranda," her grandmother called again, this time louder. The bed creaked and Miranda heard slippers shuffling on the hardwood floor.

"Yes, Grandma," she answered. "I got a drink. I'm going back to bed now."

"Okay, dear. I'll come tuck you in as soon as I get a drink myself."

Miranda kicked off her shoes, slipped out of her coat and shirt, and pulled her nightgown over her jeans. She crawled under the covers as Grandma came down the hall.

"Are you having a hard time going to sleep, Sweetie?" her grandmother asked as she sat on the edge of the bed, gently stroking Miranda's forehead.

Miranda nodded.

"Do you want to talk about it?"

"I'm just not tired," Miranda said shaking her head. "I have a headache."

The pain had started as a dull ache in the back of her head with sharp pains in her neck, but now her whole head throbbed.

Grandma got her a Tylenol and then began gently massaging Miranda's shoulders.

"No wonder your head aches. The muscles in your neck and shoulders are like steel cables," Grandma commented. "What are you so uptight about?"

Miranda just shrugged. The gentle massage felt wonderful and her headache began to fade. She closed her eyes and concentrated on the soothing touch of Grandma's hands. The next thing she knew, Grandma was shaking her.

"Are you feeling better, Miranda? It's time to get ready for school."

Mrs. Penrose stopped Miranda as the eager fifth-graders filed out for recess.

"Is something wrong today, Miranda? You don't seem to be here," she said. "I called on you several times before you heard me during reading. You haven't completed any of your assignments. What's distracting you?"

"I don't really want to talk about it," Miranda murmured, looking at the floor.

"All right, but if you change your mind, I'm here," Mrs. Penrose said softly. "In the meantime, I want you to stay in from recess and finish your math. Do you understand it?"

Miranda nodded. The math they were doing wasn't all that hard; she just couldn't concentrate on anything except how she was going to save Starlight. Later that afternoon, she even turned down Laurie's offer to play after school.

"I have to get right home," she lied.

"Really?" Laurie asked, hurt and suspicion in her voice and eyes.

"No," Miranda admitted, looking at the ground. "I'm sorry. I didn't mean to lie to you. I'm going to go across the field as soon as everyone leaves after school. Mr. Taylor will probably kill me if he sees me, but I just can't wait any longer."

"Are you sure? They say if he sees anyone in his field he calls the cops, no matter who it is! And there are no trees or anything to hide behind."

"I know, but I have to take the chance. It would take too long to walk around on the road."

"Do you want me to go with you?" Laurie's eyes were wide with fear.

"Thanks, Laurie, but I don't think that's a good idea. Two would be more noticeable than one and you'd be in trouble, too, if Mr. Taylor saw us."

Miranda breathed a sigh of relief when she made it to the old barn without being seen. The barn looked deserted so she walked through it to the corral. She looked around before hurrying toward the stables. When she heard a vehicle coming, she ran to the watering trough and crouched behind it. A pickup stopped on the other side of the trough.

"Higgins, don't be spending all your time doctoring that horse," she heard Cash Taylor say. "Doc

Talbot says that even if he lives through this, he'll be too crippled to race and too scarred for show. I've called the rendering company to put him down and haul him off, but they can't come until Saturday. I'd have the vet put him out of his misery now, but I don't want a dead horse lying around for the rest of the week until they can get here."

Miranda remembered that Grandpa had called the rendering company when one of their cows got sick and died. A few hours later, a big truck had come, loaded it up and hauled it away.

Peeking around the water trough, Miranda could only see Higgins. He was short, thin, and stooped. His voice was as thin as his wispy gray hair. Miranda couldn't make out what he was saying.

"I don't like it any better than you do, Higgins," Cash Taylor shouted. In a lower voice he added, "If you think he's suffering too much, go ahead and put a bullet in his head."

Miranda pulled her head back when she heard the pickup start again. For a moment, it sounded as if it were driving into the corral, but then it stopped and backed up. She held her breath until the sound faded in the distance. Peering around the edge of the trough again, she watched Higgins walk slowly down the stable row toward the bunkhouse. When he was out of sight, she hurried to Starlight's stall.

It took her eyes a moment to adjust to the dim light before she saw the dark horse lying in the corner. She knelt beside him. Tears flooded her eyes as she wrapped her arms around his neck. He tried to get to his feet and she stood back, talking softly.

"No, no. Don't hurt yourself. It's okay, boy. I won't hurt you," she paused to wipe tears from her eyes. "I guess I did hurt you, but I didn't mean to. I love you, and I won't ever hurt you again. I won't let them kill you, either. You don't want to die. I can tell you don't."

She examined him closely now. There was a long diagonal gash across his chest, but it wasn't very deep. It had been washed and some kind of salve was smeared on it. His left upper leg and shoulder were raked with deeper gashes. They were oozing blood, turned orange by the yellow salve that mixed with it as it ran down his leg.

"Oh, your bandage fell off," Miranda said, picking up a blood soaked piece of gauze and tape. "I'm so sorry, Starlight. This looks painful. Still, I don't see why these wouldn't heal with a few stitches. Sure it's ugly but not deep enough to cripple you. It's just like Mr. Taylor to want to get rid of you just because you're going to have a few scars. Well, I don't care what you look like. I'll always love you."

Miranda slipped out and got some grain for him. He sniffed it but wouldn't eat. His muzzle seemed warm, and liquid seeped from his nostrils.

"You've got to drink, Starlight. I think you have a fever and drinking lots of water will help."

She noticed that Higgins had left a bucket of water on the floor near the colt. She scooted it under his nose, but he turned his head away, knocking the pail over. When the cold water hit his chest he made a halfhearted attempt to stand up.

Miranda grabbed his bucket and went to fill it. She stopped in the tack shed to get more bandages. Searching through the array of liniments, salves, and vet supplies, she found something in a big yellow tube that looked and smelled like the medicine on Starlight's chest. When she came back, he was standing and she saw that a bandage on his right hind pastern, just above the hoof, was completely soaked and dirty. She'd get to that later. Opening the tube, she squeezed some salve onto a square piece of gauze and stepped closer.

The crunch of tires in the driveway made her jump and drop the greased gauze. She grabbed it, stuffed the medicine and the rest of the bandages in her pocket. Snatching up the soiled bandage, she looked for a place to hide.

As she dashed out the back of Starlight's stall and around the corner, she heard Mr. Taylor's voice.

"Hi, fellow. What are you doing up? Why the heck don't you have bandages on these deep cuts? I told Doc Talbot not to bother to stitch them, but I thought he'd put something on to staunch the bleeding. He's rebelling, I suppose, because he didn't like my decision to have you put out of your misery, but that's no excuse for not covering a wound as deep as these. He admitted you have little chance of making it, and I told him to make you as comfortable as possible. Well, I'll dress it myself."

Miranda heard the stable door close and the latch rattle. She climbed the fence and slipped into the stall next to Starlight's. It was empty. She found a knothole through the wall of Starlight's stall and sat next to it. It was warmer out of the wind and now she could see, as well as hear, Mr. Taylor.

"Can't find the Corona, but this might even do better," he said to the colt. "Easy now."

Miranda heard the hiss of a spray-can nozzle. Starlight flinched.

"If I could get hold of that girl right now, I'd rip her limb from limb. I suspected it was that fat kid of Bergman's, but Higgins said it was a girl that came running up from the pasture," Mr. Taylor muttered. "Had to be that brown haired girl the Bergman kid brought along."

Miranda was flooded with guilt. How long could she let Laurie go on taking the blame for what she had done? Mr. Taylor's angry mumbling continued, but Miranda could only understand snatches of it. "Dang barb-wire. . . Should've made sure. . . Drain the bog and get rid of every scrap of old wire. . ."

He rambled on and on in the same low rumbling monotone. Miranda wished he would leave.

"Your shavings are wet!" Mr. Taylor growled. "Let me get those out before you lie back down."

She watched him clean the stall, put down fresh shavings and try to feed the colt. Finally, he stroked Starlight's right hip and ran his hand down his leg to his ankle.

"Better change this one while I'm at it. It's completely soaked."

He worked only two feet from where Miranda peered through the knothole. She held her breath for fear he would hear her. She stared as he unwrapped

the bloody dressing and gasped when he took it off. A deep and jagged tear in the flesh just above the back of the hoof went halfway around his pastern.

Mr. Taylor looked up quickly. Miranda leaned away from the knothole and held her breath.

"Was that you, boy? It hurts, doesn't it?" Mr. Taylor droned on again. "Well, don't worry. We'll put you out of your pain. Maybe I should do it now; no sense letting you suffer. Can you stand it for two more days? Here, I'll give you another shot of Novocaine to numb the pain."

He suddenly stopped talking and Miranda thought she heard him sniffle. He left the stable and returned with a small syringe. In silence he administered the anesthetic to the two major wounds and left again. When Miranda heard his pickup start up and drive away, she crept back into Starlight's stall.

"I'm so very sorry," she whispered as tears streamed from her eyes. "You've got to hang on, boy. I'll think of something. I can't let them kill you."

She was sobbing so hard she could say no more, so she stumbled from the stable and ran across the field toward home.

It was getting dark when she reached the school, and she knew she must hurry. She had just started running down the gravel road when she saw Grandma's car coming toward her.

"Where have you been?" Grandma asked.

"Over at Shady Hills," Miranda answered, surprised at the question. Grandma was supposed to think she had gone there with Chris.

"Christopher called to talk to you, and I told him I thought you were with him," Grandma explained. "He said he didn't go to the stables today and he hadn't seen you since school."

Miranda said nothing.

"Miranda, if you were at Shady Hills, how did you get there?"

"Walked."

"That's a long walk," Grandma said.

"Not across the field."

"I gave you permission to go with Mrs. Bergman, not to go trespassing across Mr. Taylor's property on your own. If there's ever a change in the plans we agree on, I expect you to either come home on the bus or call me."

"I'm sorry. I didn't think you'd worry since you thought I'd be at Shady Hills, anyway."

"Miranda, even though you're ten years old, I don't feel comfortable having you riding without an adult around. Horses can be dangerous, you know."

Grandma must think that Mrs. Bergman stayed with them at Shady Hills. Miranda didn't correct her.

"Why did you go if Chris didn't?" Grandma wanted to know. "Did you ride his horse without his permission?"

"No!" Miranda exclaimed. "Honest, I didn't."

"Then what were you doing there?"

"Checking on the horse that got hurt."

"You could have called from home and asked

about it," Grandma said.

"But I needed to see him for myself!"

"Then you should have come home and asked me to take you," Grandma replied. In a gentler voice she asked, "How is the horse?"

"Not good. The owner doesn't think he will ever get well."

"You talked to the owner?" Grandma asked.

"No, he was busy. But I want to ask him if I can work for him, help with the horse that got hurt and do some other chores, maybe."

"I think you have enough chores to do. I want you to come home after school tomorrow."

"But, Grandma, I have to go back tomorrow to see Starlight! Besides, Chris wants me to help him with Queen."

"I'm sorry, Miranda. It's important that you learn to be responsible. I was imagining all kinds of things that might have happened to you. When I learned you weren't with Chris I was absolutely frantic. I'm responsible for your safety, but you have to let me know where you are at all times. If anything like this happens again, you'll be grounded for at least a week."

Chapter Eight

Miranda was in a stormy mood at school the next day. She refused to speak to Chris. At lunch he sat directly across from her, staring at her until she looked up.

"What's wrong with you today?" he demanded.

"You should know," Miranda retorted.

"I don't, so tell me."

"You got me in trouble with my grandma, and now I can't go with you to Shady Hills."

"I didn't get you in trouble. How was I supposed to know you weren't home?" Chris demanded. "Where were you anyway?"

"None of your business," Miranda retorted. "You don't have any reason to call me at home. Why did you?"

"Just wanted to tell you I won't be going to

ride tonight. My uncle is coming over after school."

"That's a dumb excuse for calling me at home. You can tell me things like that at school. Don't call me again unless. . . unless you, I mean unless your horse is dying!" Miranda exclaimed. "Will you be going to Shady Hills tomorrow?"

"What if I am?" Chris shouted back. "Do you think I'd take you along so I could hear you yell at me some more? Jeez you're hard to please!"

"I'm sorry. I guess it wasn't your fault I got in trouble. Please let me go."

"Well, maybe. Let's see. It's Friday, so I'm not sure what Mom has planned. If I do, will you're grandma let you go?"

"I don't know," Miranda said. "I hope so."

Miranda got busy on her chores as soon as she got home. Then she did her homework. After supper, she washed the dishes as Grandma tidied up the kitchen.

"Grandma, I'm sorry I worried you. I know I should've asked before I went to see Starlight."

"I accept your apology, Miranda," Grandma said. "I hope it never happens again. Grandpa and I need your cooperation."

"I know. I'll do better," Miranda paused, then asked, "Grandma, do you think I could go with Chris after school tomorrow if he goes? I'll come right home if he doesn't."

"Is this why you've been so helpful and responsible tonight?" asked Grandma with a wry smile.

"No. Well, sort of, but mainly I felt bad about worrying you and I want you to trust me again."

"Oh, Mandy," Grandma said, hugging her. "Trust is a two way street, you know."

Touched by hearing the affectionate nickname that they had used when she was a toddler, Miranda almost cried. She snuggled into Grandma's arms.

"May I go?" Miranda finally repeated.

"I guess so, Miranda. But call me after school and let me know whether you're going or not."

"Miranda," Chris said as Mrs. Bergman turned down the lane to Shady Hills, "Mr. Taylor is going to be out of town until Monday. He went to a horse sale in Wyoming."

Miranda smiled her relief and reached for the door handle, ready to jump out as soon as the mini-van stopped. She hurried to Starlight's stall and crept inside. Starlight was lying down, dozing.

"Miranda," Chris called, "Come help me."

"Chris, you've got to learn to do it yourself," Miranda said impatiently. "You've done each step, now just put it all together."

"If you're not going to do anything, I'm going to quit bringing you with me."

"Fine," Miranda said, "I'll help you get her saddled."

"Please ride her first," Chris pleaded. "She might be pretty frisky after not being ridden for a while."

Miranda started to call him a wimp, but she stopped when she saw real fear in his eyes.

"Okay," she said, "if it makes you feel better."

Miranda rode into the pasture while Chris cleaned the stall.

The autumn air was fresh and clean. All signs of the early snows had disappeared, and the sun shimmered on the dancing leaves of the aspen. Miranda loved this time of year, but today there was heavi-

ness in her chest, and tears clouded the beauty around her. As she felt the responsiveness of the mare beneath her, she remembered the power of Starlight's rippling muscles as he had sped down this path. Now, he might never run again.

Bursting into tears, Miranda hunched in the saddle, sobbing. She didn't attempt to guide the mare but closed her eyes to the beauties around her. Queen followed the well-worn trail that circled back toward the stables. When they drew near the paddock, Miranda wiped her eyes, hoping Chris wouldn't guess that she had been crying.

"She's wonderful," Miranda said, handing Chris the reins. "You'll have no trouble at all."

"What's wrong with you?" Chris asked. "Your eyes are all red and you sound like you have a cold."

"Well, maybe I'm getting one," Miranda said walking away. "Just go ride."

"Aren't you going to watch me?" Chris asked.

"Why do I need to watch you?"

"What else are you going to do?" Chris asked suspiciously.

"I just want to look at the other horses," she answered, rolling her eyes in exasperation.

"You let that Jet Propelled Cadillac out of his paddock, didn't you? Did you ride him?"

"Who?" Miranda decided to play dumb.

"You know. That high powered two-year-old of Mr. Taylor's that got all cut up."

Miranda hesitated.

"You did!" Chris yelled. "I thought so. You are dead meat if Cash Taylor ever finds out!"

"Oh, Chris, please don't tell. It was an accident. I sure didn't want Starlight to get hurt!" To her dismay, Miranda couldn't stop tears from flooding her eyes and streaming down her face again.

"Jeez, Miranda, I'm not going to tell!" Chris exclaimed. "Why did you do it?"

"I didn't mean to! I love that horse more than any animal I've ever seen and now they're going to kill him, all because of me. I loved him and I killed him," Miranda sobbed. Slumping to the ground, she buried her head in her arms.

Chris sat beside her and put his arm around her shoulders.

"Jeez, Miranda," he repeated, "I won't tell, I promise."

"Oh, what does it matter?" Miranda snuffled. "I don't care what they do to me. I deserve the worst. I just want to save Starlight!"

"I don't think they'll really kill him," Chris said. "Mr. Taylor was probably just bluffing when he said he was going to sell him for dog food."

"No. He meant it. I heard him tell Higgins," Miranda said. "If I had a lot of money, I'd have a vet come look at him and tell me what to do."

"Hey, I could pay the vet. I have money and you could pay me back," Chris said.

"Really?"

"Sure!" Chris exclaimed. "There's a phone in

the tack shed."

They put Queen back in her stall, still saddled, and ran to make the call. Chris picked up the phone and Miranda looked up the number. She read it off as Chris dialed.

"Hi, is Dr. Talbot there?" Chris asked. "I need him to come look at my horse over at Shady Hills."

Miranda held her breath as Chris paused.

"Uh, a cut on her leg." He covered the mouthpiece and whispered to Miranda, "I can't tell him it's for Mr. Taylor's horse, can I?. . .What?. . .Oh, good. Thanks."

He hung up and smiled triumphantly. "He's out on a call, but she's having him stop here on his way back to town."

"We'll have to make up a story or he'll never look at Starlight," Miranda said. "He's already seen him and he knows Mr. Taylor plans to have him put to sleep."

"What can we tell him?" Chris asked.

"Tell him we talked Mr. Taylor into selling him to us." Miranda said quickly, wishing it was true. "But we have one more problem."

"What's that?" Chris asked.

Miranda told him about the conversation that she heard between Mr. Taylor and Higgins when she was hiding behind the water trough.

"We can't let the rendering company come out and put him down, but I don't know how to stop them. I don't think they'd believe us if we called and told them Mr. Taylor said not to come."

"No, everyone around here knows Taylor.

"What will we do? I can't let Starlight die. I promised him I wouldn't."

"Well, I have an uncle who might help. His voice is pretty close to Taylor's. If I can just convince him to call, they might think it was Mr. Taylor."

"Can you trust him, Chris?" asked Miranda.

"I think so. I'd have to talk to him in person when he's not busy, and I'd make him promise not to tell anyone."

"But we don't have much time. They're going to come tomorrow if we don't call them."

"I'll go over to his house tonight, I promise."

"Oh, I hope it works. If not, Starlight doesn't have a chance."

"Why do you keep calling him Starlight? Don't you even know his name?" Chris asked as they entered his stall.

"What kind of a name is Sir Jet Propelled Cadillac? I named him Starlight because he's as black as night, but he has a star that shines in the dark," she explained as she brushed back his forelock to show Chris the star.

When Dr. Talbot arrived, Chris did the talking since he had made the call.

"It's not Queen. It's this other horse that my friend and I are buying from Mr. Taylor. We talked him into selling him since he's no good for racing anymore," Chris said as he led Doctor Talbot to

Starlight's stall.

"What? Mr. Taylor was dead set on having him put out of his misery. Why would he decide to sell him? I'm surprised he's still alive!" the vet exclaimed.

"He seemed to be doing better, and we promised to take good care of him," Miranda added. "He said to call you and you'd tell us what to do."

"Well, I need to talk to Cash before I do anything more with this horse. His last orders to me were to leave him alone," Dr. Talbot said, turning back toward his truck.

"But Dr. Talbot," Chris cried, "Mr. Taylor's on his way to Wyoming for the weekend. Please don't wait until he gets back. The horse needs help now."

"Can you show me a bill of sale?"

"No, there wasn't time for that. He said he'd take care of the paperwork when he gets back," Miranda said, surprised at how easy it was to think up lie after lie; it seemed that one always led to another.

"Well, I guess it won't hurt to look," the doctor conceded. "I didn't want to give up on him anyway."

Dr. Talbot gave Starlight an antibiotic by injection and told Chris and Miranda to keep offering him water and grain. He changed the dressings and said he'd come back tomorrow to give him another shot.

"How in the world are we going to pay for this?" Miranda asked Chris when the vet had gone.

"I told him to put it on Dad's bill," Chris said. "I'll take money out of my savings and pay it before

Dad gets it."

"I have a little saved," Miranda said. "I'll give you all of that."

"Uh, oh," Chris said. "Here comes Mom and I haven't even ridden yet. Help me get the saddle off before she asks me to ride for her."

They quickly unsaddled the mare and Miranda began brushing her as Chris put the tack away.

Just as she was latching the door on Queen's stall, Miranda saw Higgins, the groom, hobbling down the alleyway between the two rows of stables. He looked as if he could hardly walk.

"Chris, what's wrong with Higgins?"

"I don't know, let's go see," and they ran toward the old man.

"It's my back," Higgins groaned. "Don't know how I'm going to get all these horses fed."

"We could help, couldn't we, Chris?"

"Mom's already mad that I wasn't ready when she got here. We gotta go, Miranda."

"Just tell her to wait until I call Grandma," Miranda said, running to the tack shed.

"Go on without me, Chris," Miranda called a moment later. "Grandma said she'll come get me. I'm going to help Higgins do the feeding."

Chapter Nine

"Who are you, anyway?" the old groom asked.

"I'm Miranda Stevens," she said, "a friend of Chris Bergman's."

"I've watched you ride," Higgins said. "You're good. I've also seen you going in and out of Sir Jet's stall."

Miranda caught her breath. Had he seen her ride Starlight into the pasture? Did he blame her for his injuries? If he knew all she had done, he would surely hate her, she thought.

"Wasn't that the vet's truck leaving?"

Miranda nodded.

"Cash told him he didn't need to come back to work on Sir Jet anymore. What was he here for?"

"Chris called him," Miranda said. She began thinking of what she could make up about Queen being sick.

"Something wrong with Queen?" the groom asked. His old eyes seemed to look into her very soul, daring her to lie.

"No, we called him for Starlight. We just can't let him die. I promised him I wouldn't."

"Promised who?"

"Starlight."

"Starlight, huh," Higgins grunted. "That's a prettier name for the lad than Sir Jet Propelled Cadillac, isn't it?"

"Yes."

"Tell you what, young lady," Higgins said. "Mr. Taylor's going to be hopping mad when he gets back and sees that his plans have been thwarted. You'll have to answer to him."

"I will," Miranda said, looking at the ground, "if he'll listen to me."

"Well, if you're going to save this horse, you'd better find a way to make him listen. In the meantime you'd better stop the rendering company or your Starlight will be gone by tomorrow night."

"Oh, Mr. Higgins, would you call them? You know they'd never listen to me," Miranda said.

"Just Higgins will do. Nobody calls me Mr. and it doesn't feel right."

"Okay, I'll try to remember, just Higgins, but do you think you could. . . ?"

"You want me to lose my job?" Higgins interrupted. "By the way, what did you tell Talbot to get him to look at Sir Jet after Cash gave orders to put him down?"

"We told him we're buying him from Mr. Taylor and that Mr. Taylor told us to call him."

"And not a word of it's true, is it?"

Miranda started to argue, but a look into Higgins' eyes stopped her.

"No," she admitted, "but I want it to be. I'd give anything to have Starlight for my own. If he were mine, I wouldn't give up on him just because he won't be pretty or fast anymore."

"I don't think those are the only reasons Cash is putting him down. He cares more about his horses than you think," Higgins said. "Did you ask if he would sell him?"

"No. I haven't talked to him."

"Maybe you should've. It'll be too late by the time he comes home on Monday."

"Please, Mr., I mean, Higgins, please call the rendering company. Don't you see that Starlight wants to live? Don't you see he can still be a good horse? Let me talk to Mr. Taylor when he gets back. If he won't change his mind, there will always be time to put him down."

"Cash Taylor isn't the easiest person to talk to, especially if he's mad at you to begin with, which I suspect he just might be. But let's do these chores so you can go home. In the meantime, I'll think about calling the rendering company."

Miranda worked harder and faster than she had ever worked before. Higgins watched as she carried hay and grain and filled water troughs.

"Don't expect Mr. Taylor to pay you for all of this. I don't know what he'll say about me letting you tend to his horses," Higgins warned.

"I don't want any money," Miranda quickly assured him. "I love horses and I like this work. Besides, I have to come back to take care of Starlight."

After she phoned Grandma to come get her, Miranda ran to Starlight's stall. She knelt beside him and stroked his face and neck as she talked softly to him.

"Starlight, I'm so sorry I hurt you! I should never have tried to ride you that day; I should've made sure the gate was latched. I'll do anything I can to save you and make you well. I don't know what Mr. Taylor will do to me, but I won't let him have you destroyed! How could he want to kill you? How could he? Starlight, please, get strong enough to walk so I can take you away from Mr. Taylor."

Miranda stood when she heard a car rumble across the cattle guard. Starlight nickered softly and bobbed his head.

"I think he likes you." A soft voice said from the darkened doorway.

Miranda gasped, "Higgins! How long have you been standing there?"

"Just came to say I called off the rendering company. I may get fired, but maybe it's time I retired anyway. I know it is, if my back doesn't get better."

"Oh, thank you!" Miranda exclaimed as tears

unexpectedly stung her eyes.

A car crunched to a stop just outside the stable.

"Miranda?" Grandma called.

"I'm coming, Grandma," Miranda answered as she wiped her eyes. She gave Starlight a kiss on the nose before she went out and closed the stall door behind her. Higgins was already halfway to the car.

"Name's Higgins, Ma'am," he said tipping his hat to Grandma. "Thanks for letting her stay to help. Couldn't have done it myself with this bad back. She's a good little worker."

"You're welcome, Mr. Higgins. I'm Kathy Greene. What happened to your back? Did you fall?"

"Just Higgins, please. No, I didn't fall. It's just the old sciatica acting up again. It happens now and then when I twist the wrong way, throwing hay or shoveling horse litter."

Or trying to get a horse out of a bog, Miranda thought, as she scrambled into the front seat beside Grandma and peered into Higgins' face. He winked as he stepped back from the car.

"See you tomorrow, Miranda," he called as Grandma backed the car away.

"Tomorrow?" Grandma asked.

"Yes, I want to help while his back is bad. Please, may I, Grandma?"

"If you do your chores early, I'll drive you over. Maybe I can take the poor man to a doctor," Grandma said. "Oh, wait; I forgot. Your mom called this evening and said she'd call back before noon tomorrow to talk to you. I told her you'd be home."

"Oh, Grandma, please don't make me wait for the phone call," Miranda begged. "Higgins can't do all the work by himself."

"Well, I guess I can have her call later."

"Thanks, Gram!" Miranda kissed Grandma on the cheek.

Miranda went immediately to Starlight's stall when she arrived early the next morning. She was able to get him to nibble some grain from her hand. She brushed him and brought him fresh water, all the time talking to him in a soothing voice. She was careful not to discuss any secrets, though, and kept looking at the doorway for Higgins. She wished she could tell him everything. Maybe she would. It would be so much easier if a grown-up knew. Doctor Talbot showed up before Higgins did.

"Well, well," the vet said. "He's looking pretty perky this morning. After I give him another shot, we might try to get him up. Don't want him to get stiff."

It didn't take much coaxing to get Starlight to his feet. Dr. Talbot let Miranda help him change the dressings.

"You're doing a good job of keeping him clean," the vet said. "Now if we can just get enough antibiotics in him to keep the infection from spreading, he might stand a chance."

"Morning, Doctor," greeted Higgins from the door to the stall.

"Hello, Higgins," the vet answered. "What do you know about the deal between Taylor and these kids? I could hardly believe Cash agreed to sell him."

Miranda held her breath as her eyes met Higgins'. Higgins raised his eyebrows at Miranda as he answered, "Whatever they work out with Mr. Taylor is none of my affair, but I'm mighty glad to see the horse getting better."

"Me too, Higgins, me too," said Dr. Talbot as

he picked up his bag. "I'll be back this afternoon to give him another injection."

Higgins' back was worse than ever. He couldn't even sit on a hay bale so he leaned on the fence as he instructed Miranda on the morning chores. She cleaned out stalls, forking the soiled shavings into a wheelbarrow to haul to a pile at the end of the long stable row.

"Why do you use shavings for bedding?" Miranda asked. "Grandpa has always used straw."

"Mr. Taylor grew up on one of the biggest horse ranches in Texas. That was the way they did it there, so, to him, that's the only way," Higgins said. "I think it absorbs moisture better."

He shifted his weight and grimaced, clutching his back.

"You really ought to go to a doctor about your back," Miranda said. "Grandma would drive you, if you want."

"My nephew, John, knows a bone-cracker he wants me to see. The chiropractor is just down the street from John's house in Bozeman and he's agreed to give the treatments on the weekend, one this afternoon and one tomorrow. John's coming soon to get me, but thanks for the offer," Higgins answered. Looking at Miranda, he added, "If you think you can handle the chores tomorrow, I'll just stay overnight at John's."

Miranda was surprised that he thought her capable and would put her in charge.

QUEEN

"Oh, yes. I can do the feeding and watering and clean stalls too!" Miranda exclaimed with pride.

"I believe you can, but you'll have to cut the hay bales where they are and haul them in the wheel barrow," Higgins said. Smiling, he added, "Here comes your business partner. If you need anything, I'll be in the bunkhouse until John comes."

"Business partner?" Miranda asked, puzzled.

Higgins nodded at the Bergman's mini-van coming down the hill, and said with a wry smile. "Or should I say, 'Partner in crime?'"

"No, business partner sounds better," Miranda said, blushing.

"Hey, Miranda," Chris called, hurrying toward her. "How's Starlight?"

"What are you doing here on Saturday? I thought you already put in your riding requirements for the week," Miranda said.

Chris grabbed her arm and said, "Miranda, you've got to help me! Mom and Dad filled out the entries for me to compete in the horse show. Mom is taking them to Bozeman the next time she goes."

"What did they enter you in?" asked Miranda.

"English Pleasure and Jumping."

"Why didn't you tell them you didn't want to enter?" asked Miranda.

"Believe me, I told them. I gave them every argument I could think of," Chris replied.

"Except the truth," Miranda teased.

"You have no right to preach to me about telling the truth," Chris said. "I've heard you lie about a lot of things. And then you have me lying for you. By the way, I didn't get a chance to talk to my uncle. Besides, I know he wouldn't do it. Sorry."

"That's okay. I got it worked out."

"Really? How?"

"Higgins called and canceled the order."

"No kidding? Wow!" Chris said. "What did you tell him?"

"The truth. At least part of it. I guess sometimes it works better than lying," Miranda said thoughtfully. "Come on, we have a lot of work to do if you're going to be ready for the show."

Miranda paid close attention to Chris as he rode around the arena. She definitely owed him for getting the veterinarian for Starlight.

"Don't hold your hands so high. Don't pull back and kick her at the same time. You're confusing her."

After an hour Chris was ready to quit.

"I am getting a side-ache from bouncing around up here," he complained.

"That's because you aren't using your legs enough. Think of them as springs. Let them bend to absorb the motion," Miranda instructed.

"Miranda, my legs are beginning to feel like spaghetti. I don't think they can hold me up another minute."

"Okay," Miranda said. "Get down for awhile and help me set up some jumps."

"Oh, no! No jumps today. I'm not ready," Chris argued.

"If you don't get started, you won't be ready by show time," Miranda said as she held the mare.

Chris slid off the horse and fell to the ground as his legs buckled under him.

"My legs are dead!" he cried.

"They'll wake up," Miranda said, laughing as she extended a hand to help him to his feet.

Together they set up some low jumps.

"That's too high to start with," Chris said.

He lowered it until it was only ten inches off the ground.

"She'll just step over that," Miranda complained. "She's a tall horse. Put it back up to at least two feet."

"Well, you're going first, so put it wherever you want to. When I get on they'll have to be lowered."

Miranda had never jumped hurdles before except for an unexpected leap over a ditch when she rode her grandfather's horse. It had been a little frightening, but she hadn't fallen off. After the first time, she crossed the ditch many times just for the fun of sailing through the air.

Miranda was thrilled to ride Queen over the jumps. The horse was a natural. All Miranda had to do was lean forward and keep her balance. Each time she jumped, she felt as if she were flying. After three times around the arena, she took the horse to Chris and lowered the hurdles for him.

"Just let her have her head, Chris," Miranda said. "Kind of lean forward and keep your balance."

Miranda noticed sweat on Chris's forehead. His mouth was set in a tight line on his pale face.

Seeing his fear made Miranda a little nervous. She watched as he trotted Queen around the arena.

"Let her canter," Miranda called.

Chris looked frozen in the saddle as he approached the first hurdle. Queen lengthened her stride and prepared to jump, but Chris jerked back on the reins. Confused, the mare stopped abruptly and shied sideways. Chris continued forward, leaving the saddle as if in slow motion, doing a flip in the air and landing on his back on the other side of the jump.

Miranda ran to his side.

"Chris, are you all right?"

He didn't answer but gasped for air.

"Why did you pull her back?" Miranda asked as Chris struggled to sit up.

As soon as he could speak he shouted, "I just can't do this! I won't ride over a jump. My parents will just have to kill me if they don't like it."

When they emerged from the indoor arena they saw Dr. Talbot's truck in the driveway. Miranda handed Chris Queen's reins and ran to Starlight's stall.

"He's looking a little better," the vet told her. "He stood when I gave him his shot. I dressed his wounds and got him to eat a little grain. The shallower wounds on his chest and shoulder are already beginning to heal."

Starlight nuzzled Miranda as she gently stroked his neck. While he was standing, she quickly forked out the soiled shavings and evenly spread what was left. With a little groan, Starlight lay down. Miranda sat beside him and cradled his head in her lap.

"Looks like you have a friend. Lucky for the horse you decided to rescue him," said the doctor, smiling. "He may never win a race, but with all the tender, loving care you're giving him, he should have a lot of useful years ahead of him."

Miranda was silent, a lump of fear jamming her throat. What if Mr. Taylor refused to save him? Starlight leaned his head against her chest.

"You're going to be all right, boy. I won't let anyone kill you." She whispered, hoping she could keep that promise.

Chapter Ten

As Miranda sat beside Starlight, eating the lunch she had brought, Higgins came to give her further instructions for the next day. Miranda walked with him to the car where his nephew held the door open for him. She cringed in sympathy when she saw the pain on Higgins' face as he eased himself into the low sports car.

After they left, Miranda sat with Starlight a little longer, talking softly as she cradled his head in her lap. She gently petted him until time to do the afternoon feeding. She'd just finished when Mrs. Bergman came for Chris and offered Miranda a ride home. After checking on Starlight, and giving him one last pat on the neck, she joined Chris in the back seat of the mini-van.

As they drove out, Mrs. Bergman asked, "Well, Chris, how was Queen today? Are you ready for the horse show?"

"Uh, she did okay, but we still have some things to work on," he answered.

"Daddy and I can hardly wait to watch you perform. We just know you'll shine! Oh, I forgot to tell you; when I turned in the entry, they talked me into adding a couple of things," Mrs. Bergman said. "You'll be in Western Pleasure and a trail class that sounds like a lot of fun. I think you need a western saddle for both those events so Daddy's getting you one today. You can try it out tomorrow."

"Mom!" Chris exclaimed. "Why didn't you ask me first? I don't have time to practice for all that."

"Oh, you silly boy!" Mrs. Bergman said, smiling into the rear view mirror, "I'm sure you're underestimating yourself. You've got the English riding down and you still have almost four months to practice for the Western events. All you have to do for the trail class is ride around a course, doing simple things like opening and closing gates, backing her between some barrels, crossing bridges, and taking things out of a mail box, all without dismounting."

Chris groaned. Miranda waited for him to tell his mother what he had told her; that he would not ride over any jumps. He said nothing, however, as he turned to look out the side window. Miranda saw a tear slide down his cheek.

Miranda finished her chores before breakfast the next morning and fixed a sandwich to take with her. She cleared the table and started washing dishes before Grandma and Grandpa were even through eating.

"What's the big rush, Miranda?" Grandma asked.

"I told Higgins I'd do the feeding again because his back is so bad." Miranda suddenly realized she hadn't actually asked them if she could go. "Please, may I go?"

"Are the Bergmans going to be there?"

"Yeah," Miranda said. "They're getting a new western saddle for Chris."

"Must be a pretty exciting job," Grandpa said, reaching for his hat. "Well, I'm going over to help Jerry Smith with his old truck. If you're ready, I can drop you off at Shady Hills on the way."

"Get your jacket," Grandma told her. "I'll finish the dishes. Call me if you need any help and let me know when you get finished this afternoon, so I can come get you."

Miranda was surprised to find Chris already mucking out Queen's stall.

"Why didn't you tell her?" Miranda asked, startling him.

"Jeez, Miranda, don't scare me like that. Tell who what?"

"Sorry. Did you tell your mom you're not going to ride in the show."

"I can't."

"What do you mean, you can't?" Miranda asked. "You say you can't ride so what choice do you have?"

"I wanted to tell her but she just kept on and on about how proud she is of me. She'd have a fit! I don't want to hear her scream and cry. Then she'd tell Dad, and he would. . ." Chris didn't finish.

"Who are you most afraid of, your parents or your horse?" Miranda demanded.

"I don't know," Chris moaned. "Hey, I have an idea. Maybe I could break my leg and then I couldn't ride." He paused and frowned as if serious about the idea. "Or maybe I could just pretend I got hurt."

"Chris Bergman!" Miranda said, laughing. "You're the biggest wimp I know."

Chris didn't answer, so she added, more seriously, "You need to either decide to ride and start working on it or give it up. I have work to do."

Chris grabbed her arm and spun her around as she turned to walk away. His face was red and his fists tightly clinched.

"Don't call me a wimp! Let's see how brave you are tomorrow when Cash Taylor comes back. How'd you like me to tell him that you're the one who let his precious horse out?"

Miranda was frightened by the look in his eyes.

"I'm sorry, Chris. I didn't mean it. I know you're trying. You'd be a good rider if you would just relax. It's just hard for me to understand why you're so afraid of horses."

Chris unclenched his fists, turned his back to her and picked up the pitchfork.

"Please don't tell Mr. Taylor," Miranda begged softly. "I may have to tell him myself, soon, but right now I'm scared to death to even let him see me."

"Now who's the wimp?" Chris asked; his voice was cold and harsh.

"Sorry I called you that, Chris. I guess I'm a worse coward than anyone. I'm constantly afraid Mr. Taylor will pop up out of nowhere and see me here. It's been a big relief to know he's out of town. For the first time since I've been here, I can breathe and enjoy myself instead of always being ready to run and hide."

"Well, I guess we're both going to have to face our fears sooner or later. Taylor will be back tomorrow, and he's going to be furious when he sees Starlight's still here," Chris said. "At least I have a few more months to either learn to ride or tell my parents the truth."

Miranda swallowed hard and nodded as a knot of fear welled up inside her. She hurried to Starlight's stall and found him on his feet, eating grain. He nickered at her as she approached. She patted his neck and checked the wounds on his chest. The bandages were soaked and dirty. She changed them, cleaning the wound and applying more medicine, just as she had seen the vet do. She was cleaning his stall when Dr. Talbot arrived.

"You're doing a fine job, young lady," Dr. Talbot said. "Just a few more days of antibiotics and I

can quit giving him shots everyday."

As soon as Dr. Talbot left, Chris called to her. He was leading Queen, saddled and bridled, to the arena. Miranda ran after them.

"Good job, Chris," Miranda said. "Did you get the cinch tight enough? I mean billet as Laurie calls it."

"See for yourself."

Miranda checked it. "Perfect," she said.

Chris was shaking when he mounted Queen, yet he didn't ask her to ride first.

"Let me take her around a few times slowly before I try any jumps," he said.

Miranda watched him. "You're doing great, Chris. I'll go get the feeding done for Higgins and then I'll come back and set up jumps for you."

He nodded as he continued around the ring.

When she returned an hour later, she asked, "Are you ready?"

"No. I don't think I'll ever be ready, but I suppose I should try."

Miranda set up one jump only eighteen inches off the ground. Chris dismounted and handed the reins to Miranda.

"Let me watch you first so I can try to get the motions right."

"Just be with the horse, Chris. Don't try to fight her."

Miranda took Queen over the hurdle.

"Put it higher. She can step over that one," she told Chris.

The next time she took the jump it was as smooth as sailing on a cloud. She jumped two more times before taking the mare back to Chris.

"Just stay with her and don't pull back. Lean forward and let her jump," Miranda called as Chris rode toward the jump.

The first time, he guided her around the jump and brought her to a stop.

"Come on, Chris!" Miranda shouted. "You can do it. I have to get back to work, so hurry up and take a jump."

The next time around, he let the mare jump the hurdle, but his eyes were closed tightly while he hunched forward, clinging to a handful of mane. Queen landed softly but Chris bounced forward, his face slamming into her mane. He quickly pulled her to a stop.

"I did it!" he exclaimed excitedly. "Did you see that, Miranda? I did it!"

"Yeah, great job. Now try it again with your eyes open. Relax a little more."

Chris rode Queen over the low jump three more times, each one a little more smoothly than the one before.

"Want me to raise it for you?" Miranda asked.

"No," Chris answered, sliding to the ground. "That's enough for one day. I have time to work up gradually. I'll help you clean stalls since you helped me."

As they forked wood chips into the wheelbarrow, Miranda asked, "What makes you so afraid of horses, Chris? It seems harder for you than I thought it would be."

"I'm not sure, Miranda. I have nightmares about them. I just see big hooves and flaring nostrils. In my dream, I'm always falling. All I know is it really scares me to ride."

"Well, you're learning. I think you have courage."

"Thanks," Chris murmured, flashing her an

embarrassed grin before turning away.

When the last stall was clean, Chris and Miranda ate their lunches in the hayloft of the old barn. When they were through eating, Chris returned to feed and groom Queen, and Miranda hurried to Starlight's stall and brushed him gently. She redressed all the wounds, using up most of the bandages. She'd have to get some more with the little money she had saved for Christmas, she decided.

She wanted to see if he could walk any distance so she opened the door to his paddock. He hobbled out behind her and stood contentedly in the bright afternoon sun.

"Good boy, Starlight," Miranda crooned. "You're getting stronger every day. I'll let you stand here so I can get your stall all the way clean."

She tied him to the fence and began forking the dirty shavings into the wheelbarrow she'd parked just outside the front door. She was just turning to carry out a fork full of dirty shavings when a dark form filled the doorway.

"What the devil are you doing here?"

Losing her grip on the pitchfork, Miranda stepped back, numb with fear.

"What horse is out there?" Cash Taylor asked as he strode across the stall. "What in tarnation is going on here? I ordered that horse put to sleep!" he shouted, shaking his fist. "Don't go anywhere, young lady. You have a lot of explaining to do, but first I'm calling the rendering company to find out why they didn't follow my orders to come get this horse."

"B-B-But, sir, wait," Miranda began.

Striding angrily across the stall, Mr. Taylor tripped over the pitchfork Miranda had dropped. He lurched forward and struck his head on the side of the door with a resounding thud. Crumpling to the ground, he lay motionless.

Chapter Eleven

Miranda stared at the still form on the stall floor. She half expected Mr. Taylor to jump up and attack her, but when he didn't move, she rushed to his side.

"Oh, Mr. Taylor, are you all right? Mr. Taylor, please don't be dead," Miranda screamed. "Chris! Chris, come quick!"

"Miranda, what's the matter?" Chris asked as he ran to Starlight's stall. "My gosh, Miranda, what did you do to him?"

"Nothing! I mean, I don't know. He's still breathing, his heart's still beating, but he doesn't move," Miranda cried. "Chris, you've got to get help. Call 911."

Chris disappeared quickly. Miranda tried to turn Mr. Taylor's twisted neck to a more comfortable position. She pulled on his feet, straightening out his back and then returned to his head. Now his face was in the shavings. She managed to turn his head to one side and gasped. A big gash on his temple was bleeding and swollen.

"Miranda, the phone is out. I don't know what's wrong, but it's dead."

"Oh, no! I'm afraid he'll die. Please go for help, Chris. Ride Queen."

Chris's face paled, but he looked at Mr. Taylor's bleeding head and nodded.

"Okay," he said. "I guess it's a good thing I didn't unsaddle her yet."

Miranda heard the sharp clip of Queen's hooves as Chris guided her past the stables and urged her to a trot, then a gallop. Miranda ran out to intercept him.

"Chris, not that way. It'd be faster to go across the field."

He didn't hear her as he cantered up the driveway. She had never seen him ride so fast.

"The cattle guard!" Miranda yelled as she saw Chris approaching the wide span of spaced pipes that allowed cars to cross, but would break the horse's leg if she stepped into it. The gate beside it was closed. Miranda held her breath in horror as Queen slowed momentarily and then ran straight toward the five-feet-high metal gate, sailing over it without breaking stride. Chris bounced forward but stayed with her, and they disappeared over the hill.

Leaning against the stable wall for support,

Miranda let out a long sigh of relief. Shaking, she slipped back into the stable.

Mr. Taylor didn't move. A few shavings stuck to his face. Hurrying to the tack shed, she found a clean cloth and soaked it in cold water at the hydrant. Kneeling beside the still form in the stall, she cautiously wiped the old man's face. Mr. Taylor moaned.

"Oh, Mr. Taylor, please wake up. Please be all right," Miranda murmured.

He groaned again and his eyes fluttered.

"What happened?" Mr. Taylor asked groggily. "Owww! My head. Where am I?"

"Mr. Taylor, you bumped your head on the door frame. You've got an awful lump on your head," Miranda said. "Please don't move. I'm afraid your neck might be broken and it's all my fault."

But Mr. Taylor rolled over and sat up.

"Nothing wrong with my neck," he said. "But my head! I can't see straight. Help me to the house!"

"Maybe you should wait. Chris went for help. He's getting an ambulance," Miranda said, afraid Mr. Taylor would keel over any minute.

"Don't argue! Help me up. I'm not going to lie here in horse litter! Get me to my sofa."

Miranda helped him to his feet. He rested his hands on her shoulder and she held on to his waist. He was very unsteady.

"Problem is, I can't see!" Mr. Taylor complained. "Everything is a big, dark blur."

Miranda bit her lip to keep from crying. She lead him past the barn and up to the front door of the house.

"The door's locked," she said as she tried in vain to twist the doorknob.

"Shoot," he muttered. "I always use the side door. Are my keys in my pocket?" He felt his pockets with his right hand. The left one still gripped Miranda's shoulder.

"No keys! We'll have to go around to the side of the house."

The side door swung inward when Miranda pushed and they stepped into a large, immaculate kitchen.

"Go this way," Mr. Taylor said, pointing to the dining room. Through an archway across the dining room, Miranda could see sofas, chairs and polished tables.

"This way," Mr. Taylor said sharply, squeezing her shoulder even harder. "In there."

He guided Miranda to a door into a dark room. Half afraid, she stepped through the door with Mr. Taylor still leaning heavily on her. He flipped on a light switch to reveal a long, narrow room with a TV at one end and a piano at the other. Heavy drapes covered a window across from the doorway. In the middle of the room were two sofas, back to back. A pillow and a quilt lay on the far one that faced the TV. Mr. Taylor eased himself onto it.

"Now, go to the kitchen and get some ice for my head," he ordered.

When Miranda came back with the ice, Mr. Taylor was pulling his quilt up under his chin. He was shivering from head to toe.

"Go get me some more blankets from the bedroom. I'm freezing," he yelled. "And get that ice away from me! I just told you, I'm cold!"

Dropping the bag of ice she'd wrapped in a dish towel, Miranda ran in search of the bedroom. When she returned with a large quilt and a wool blanket, Mr. Taylor's eyes were closed and his teeth were chattering. She tucked the blankets around him.

He lay quietly without a word for a few minutes. She stared hard at him to see if he was breathing, holding her own breath until she finally saw his chest rise. At last he opened one eye.

"Who the heck are you? What are you doing here?" he growled, as if seeing her for the first time. "I want you out of my house and off my property!

"But, I can't leave you like this," Miranda said softly. "Help should be coming soon."

"Was I dreaming, or is Sir Jet still alive and on his feet out there?"

"Yes, he is."

"Give me that phone. I have to call the rendering company and see why they didn't follow my orders. He should have been put out of his misery and hauled away yesterday. Then I'll give you ten seconds to clear out of here before I call the cops."

"Please wait. I can explain everything."

"Get me the darn phone!" Mr. Taylor shouted, raising menacingly on his elbow.

Miranda found a phone on the desk behind the couch and handed it to him .

"I don't think it works, sir. The one in the tack shed didn't."

"Dead!" Mr. Taylor yelled. "What did you do to the phone?"

"Nothing," Miranda said, tears welling in her eyes. "You don't have to yell at me. I didn't mean to hurt you. And, I didn't mean to hurt Starlight. I love him and would never hurt him on purpose!" Sobbing, Miranda fell to her knees beside the sofa where Mr. Taylor lay staring at her as if he thought she'd gone crazy. "I can't let you kill him. I'll work hard and pay you however much you ask, but you can't kill him. You'll have to kill me first." Miranda's voice rose uncontrollably as tears streamed down her face, but she looked straight into Mr. Taylor's eyes.

"Who the devil is Starlight, and what are you talking about?" Mr. Taylor demanded. "Have you lost your mind?"

"No! Starlight is that beautiful colt you want to have killed. You gave up on him just because he couldn't make you rich," shouted Miranda, rising to her feet. "You don't care about him. You only care about the money he could've made for you. Can't you see he wants to live? I promised him I wouldn't let him die."

Mr. Taylor looked at her without a word. His face was the color of cement except for the ugly red welt that was getting larger by the minute. Miranda trembled under his gaze.

"My vision's clearing up a bit. Come closer so I can see who you are."

Miranda breathed sharply and hesitated. Then she slowly knelt beside the sofa again, until her face was two feet from his.

"John Greene's kid, right?" Mr. Taylor didn't wait for her to answer. "You're a troublemaker from the word go, aren't you?"

"I don't mean to be."

"Riding horses that don't belong to you; coming onto my place when I told you to stay off. Messing with my horse like he belonged to you. Then you nearly killed me. You don't call that causing trouble?"

"Yes, I do, and I'm sorry, but I never meant to hurt anyone." Miranda took a deep breath and rushed on. "I came to help Chris with his horse. I didn't know it was your place 'til I got here. Then I saw Starlight and I just had to come back, but I didn't mean to hurt him. I didn't mean to hurt you either. You scared me so bad I dropped the pitchfork. That's what you tripped over."

Mr. Taylor shuddered and closed his eyes. "I'm too tired to make sense out of all your blubbering. Would you just go away?"

"Mr. Taylor, I'm awfully sorry, but I have to stay until the ambulance comes. I have to talk to you about Starlight. Please don't kill him. He's getting stronger every day."

Miranda jumped up suddenly. "Oh, no! I forgot to put him back in the stall."

She ran out the door and raced to the stable, scolding herself all the way. How could she have forgotten him for so long? She tried to remember how she had tied him. If he became too tired to stand and tried to lie down, would the rope allow it? She imagined him hanging by his halter, his life seeping from him. What a relief it was to see he was still on his feet beyond the back door.

Starlight nickered to her as she rushed in and called his name. She ran out the back door and threw her arms around him before standing back to look him over carefully. He seemed to be all right, so she quickly spread clean shavings on the floor before leading him inside. He went to his water trough, took a long drink and, after  turning in a circle, nose to the ground, sank into the fresh shavings with a groan. Miranda put a flake of hay under his nose and offered him a handful of grain. He mouthed it halfheartedly.

"I love you, Starlight," she whispered as she slipped off his halter and patted his neck.

Mr. Taylor seemed to be sleeping when Miranda returned. His face was ashen and cold. She picked up the quilt that had fallen on the floor and tucked it in around his shoulders. He breathed unevenly but didn't open his eyes.

Miranda wandered nervously around the room. On the piano was a black and white portrait of a little girl about her age. She had long, dark ringlets and large, sober eyes. Nervously, Miranda went to the living room and peered out the window. Why wasn't the ambulance here yet? She hoped Chris was all right. What if he were lying unconscious along the road somewhere? She strained harder to see down the lane. It was almost dark now. Queen would come home if she'd lost her rider, wouldn't she?"

"Girlie? I need some water. Are you here?" Mr. Taylor's raspy voice made her jump.

As she looked for a glass, Miranda noticed the telephone on the kitchen counter top. The receiver rested on its cradle at a rakish angle with the cord caught between. She put the receiver to her ear and jiggled the hook on the cradle. Dial tone!

"What's taking you so long?" Mr. Taylor shouted, "Hurry up with that water!"

She quickly filled a glass, hurried back to the den and knelt beside the couch.

He drank slowly as she supported his head.

"That's enough," he said, lying back down.

"You feeling better?" Miranda asked hopefully.

"Some."

Miranda felt the uncomfortable silence as the old man stared at the ceiling. Maybe she should go back to the kitchen and phone 911. They should have been here by now. She stood to go to the telephone.

"Did you get some ice for my head?" Mr. Taylor asked.

"Yes, it's here," Miranda said, returning to his side.

The towel was a little wet where ice had melted through holes in the plastic bag.

"Let me get a fresh bag of ice. That one's wet."

"It's fine. Feel's good. Just leave it here."

Mr. Taylor's eyes were covered with the towel, and Miranda tiptoed toward the door.

"My blankets are falling off. Would you straighten them," asked Mr. Taylor.

Miranda quickly turned around and did as he asked. *I could call from here, but then he'll know the phone works, and call the rendering company,* Miranda thought. Mr. Taylor's hand fell away from his face, pulling the towel with it. Miranda gasped. His face was deathly gray and still.

Chapter Twelve

Frozen in fear, Miranda stared at Mr. Taylor until she finally saw his chest rise. Letting her breath out slowly, she sat on the floor by his side. Maybe if she could get him to talk, she'd keep him from dying before the ambulance arrived.

"Who's the girl in the picture on the piano?" Miranda asked.

"What are you snooping around my house for?" Mr. Taylor demanded sharply, opening one eye. "I thought I told you to leave."

"I didn't mean any harm. I just happened to notice it. She reminds me of my best friend."

"Well, she isn't."

"I know she isn't, Mr. Taylor, but she's very beautiful. She must be special to you or you wouldn't have her picture."

"How do you know what I wouldn't do?"

"You don't like kids, do you?" Miranda accused.

"Why should I? They just make trouble."

"Even the one in the picture?"

"Never heard a kid talk so much. Why don't you leave me alone?"

"I just want to know." Miranda was determined to keep Mr. Taylor awake.

"It's none of your business, but she's my daughter," Mr. Taylor said. "Only she's not a kid anymore. She'd be almost forty years old by now, if she's still living."

"You don't know if she's alive?"

"Haven't seen her since that picture was taken. For a while I got a letter every month. Then her mother wouldn't let her write anymore. My ex-wife told me I just caused trouble."

"Why did you divorce your wife?" Miranda asked, hoping to understand why grownups couldn't just get along. "Didn't you love her?"

"You ask too many questions about things that don't concern you," Mr. Taylor snarled.

"My parents got divorced. I haven't seen my father since I was born. I guess he hated me."

"Now don't go making assumptions about how other people feel. I loved my wife and daughter. But my parents wouldn't leave us alone. She had been my mother's housekeeper and, therefore, beneath our social status. Yet she made me happier than I'd ever been before."

Mr. Taylor closed his eyes and was quiet so long that she began to worry, but his breathing seemed normal. Thinking he was asleep, she reached for the telephone. She jumped when he started talking again.

"She left before the baby was born. For a long time, I was furious that she went back to her home in England without even saying good-bye. My parents said she told them that she didn't love me anymore. Come to find out, they'd told her that I said I didn't love her and was sorry I married her. I finally came to my senses and went looking for them. Cassy was five years old by that time."

"Wow, that's a long time! Wouldn't she come back with you?" Miranda asked.

Mr. Taylor opened his eyes and looked at her in surprise, as if he'd forgotten she was there. He closed them again and went on.

"Jesse, my wife, wouldn't have me. She said she'd spent almost six years trying to forget me, and she wasn't going to start over again. I spent two months getting acquainted with my daughter, Cassy, and trying to get Jesse to change her mind. No such luck. I think she was already in love with someone else, because she got married the next summer. I visited them every summer until Jesse put a stop to it. According to her, I was making it hard for Cassy to bond with Jesse's new husband.

"Sometimes I wished I hadn't looked for her," Mr. Taylor said. "Now I had two women to break my heart. Cassy was almost ten the last time I saw her;

the prettiest and brightest thing I ever saw. Couldn't stand to look at a little girl after that. I'd almost forgotten her until I saw a girl that looked just like her sitting on the fence of Queen's paddock one day."

"That was my friend, Laurie."

"Well, I think she's the one who let Sir Jet out and get hurt. I gave orders for her to stay off my place. I don't need troublemakers around here. Besides I don't want to be reminded of my Cassy."

"No!" Miranda shouted.

"No, what?" Mr. Taylor opened his eyes and stared at her.

"No, Laurie isn't the one who did it. She's a wonderful person. You'd like her if you knew her."

"How do you know she didn't do it?"

"I tried to tell you; I did it." She rushed on, afraid he'd interrupt her. "But I didn't mean to. I was only going to ride him around the paddock a little. I didn't realize I left the gate open. Honestly, Mr. Taylor, I'm sorrier than anything! I love that horse." Miranda paused, glancing at Mr. Taylor's firm jaw and narrowed eyes. "Please, Mr. Taylor, don't kill Starlight. Do whatever you want to me, but don't kill him. He's a good horse, and he deserves to live."

Miranda couldn't keep back the tears so she buried her face in her hands and sobbed.

"Don't cry. For heavens sake, quit crying!" Mr. Taylor yelled. "Cassy cried like that when I left England the last time, and I just can't stand it."

"If you try to shoot him, you'll have to shoot

me first. Can't you see it's all my fault? Don't punish Starlight!" Miranda pleaded between choking sobs.

"I'm not going to kill Starlight, er, Sir Jet, I mean. I don't know what I'll do with him, but I couldn't have him put down now after seeing him standing there all bright eyed."

Miranda quit crying and stared at him.

"Oh, Mr. Taylor, thank you, thank you! Please say I can come back and take care of him. And Laurie, too. Please. We won't cause trouble, we'll only help."

The eerie whine of a distant siren broke the stillness.

"You not cause trouble? That I'd like to see," Mr. Taylor snorted. "Well, here comes your dang ambulance. Now you can finally leave. Oh, don't look at me that way. I'll think about it."

Grandpa appeared in the door of the dairy barn as Miranda jumped down from Mr. Bergman's four-wheel-drive pickup.

"Thanks for the ride, Mr. Bergman. See ya Monday, Chris."

As the Bergmans drove away, Grandpa strode quickly across the driveway to meet Miranda.

Oh, no. I forgot to call and tell them why I was late. Miranda thought. *Now I'm in big trouble.*

"Are you okay, Miranda?" Grandpa asked, stooping down to hug her.

"Yes, Grandpa. I'm fine. I'm sorry I forgot to call, but the phone was out for a while and there was so much going on."

"Where's your Grandmother?"

"What do you mean? Isn't she in the house?"

"She went looking for you an hour ago. We expected you to call us to come get you, Miranda. It's almost seven o'clock."

"I was at Shady Hills all the time. I don't know why she didn't find me."

"Well, I expect she'll be along soon. I've finished the milking and just have to clean the barn. Come in and help me. I think we need to talk."

Miranda followed Grandpa into the barn where the milkers were already being flushed and cleaned. Grandpa picked up the high-pressure hose and started washing down the concrete floor. Miranda grabbed the big floor broom and started sweeping, well aware of the firm set of Grandpa's jaw and his knitted brow.

"Well, Miranda," Grandpa began at last, as he turned off the hose. "Start by explaining what happened tonight to keep you from calling us. You must have known that we'd be worried."

"There was an accident. Mr. Taylor fell and hit his head. It knocked him out. I had to help him."

"Why didn't you call?"

"The phone didn't work. Chris rode his horse to get help because we couldn't even call 911."

"Where was Mrs. Bergman? Wasn't she there with her car?"

"No, she had already left. It was just Chris and

me. And Mr. Taylor."

"Doesn't Mrs. Bergman stay with you kids when you ride?"

"Well, not always," Miranda murmured looking at her feet.

"Miranda?" Grandpa lifted Miranda's chin until her eyes met his.

"Well, no. She just drops us off and then comes back to pick us up later."

"Well, we'll discuss that later. Is Mr. Taylor okay?"

"Yes, I think so. I helped him to the house and stayed with him until the ambulance came. He refused to go to the hospital."

"I want to hear the whole story from start to finish, but let's go to the house," Grandpa said, opening the door. "Oh, good. Here comes your grandma."

As Grandpa closed the door behind them, Miranda saw a pair of headlights coming up the driveway. Grandpa strode forward to meet his wife as she came to a stop. Miranda followed slowly behind.

"She's here, Honey," she heard him reassure Grandma. "She's okay."

"I know," Grandma said as she got out of the car. "Mr. Bergman told me when he stopped to help me change a flat tire."

Grandma sounded tired and irritable. Miranda escaped to the bathroom as soon as they entered the house. She leaned over the counter-top and stared into the mirror. Her cheeks were rosy from the night air,

but her eyes were wide and frightened.

"You should've called Grandma when you got the phone back on line," accused the mirror girl.

"I know. I think she's really mad."

"Miranda?" It was Grandpa's voice. "Come out as soon as you're finished. Grandma needs the bathroom, too."

Miranda unlocked the door and stepped out.

"Sorry," she said, wrapping her arms around Grandpa's narrow waist.

He patted her shoulder and hugged her back before taking her hand and leading her to the living room. He dropped wearily into his recliner and Miranda sat on the floor near his feet.

"Okay," Grandma began as she joined them. "Let me tell you what I've been through, Miranda. I need to get it off my chest before I begin questioning you. But when I do, I want no excuses, just the truth."

Miranda nodded, her eyes locked on

Grandma's stern face.

"I fully expected you to be through helping Mr. Higgins by mid-afternoon at the latest. When you hadn't called by four, I was disappointed but not really worried yet. I left the answering machine on and went out to do chores. I came in at five to see if you'd called. When there was still no message by six, I was absolutely frantic and went looking for you. I drove to Shady Hills and didn't see a soul."

"But I was there, in Mr. Taylor's house!" Miranda exclaimed.

"I thought he was out of town." Grandma didn't sound as if she believed Miranda.

"He got back early. We were in a room at the back of the house. I didn't hear anybody drive in."

"Why were you in Mr. Taylor's house, and why didn't you call me?" Grandma was almost yelling.

Grandpa said nothing as Miranda repeated what she'd already told him.

"Just how did Mr. Taylor happen to fall, and how did you find him?" Grandpa wanted to know.

"Well, he came in the stall I was cleaning and he tripped over a pitchfork."

"Was he helping you clean the stall?" asked Grandma.

"Well, no. He just came in to, uh, to look at the horse that was outside the back door."

"Why was there a pitchfork on the floor?" Grandpa was very particular about keeping such implements picked up and out of the way.

"I, uh, accidentally dropped it."

"Miranda, I want the whole story from the beginning. Don't leave anything out," Grandma said severely.

"Well, I wasn't expecting him. Mr. Taylor, I mean. When he yelled, it scared me and I dropped the pitchfork."

"Why did he yell?"

"Well, I guess he was surprised to see me."

Grandpa gently squeezed her shoulder and said, very quietly, "Look at me, Miranda. Grandma and I have long suspected that you haven't been telling us everything. I want to know why you keep things from us. Oh, we don't expect you to tell us everything you do, say, or think, but we expect you to let us help you with your problems. I don't want any more lies, Miranda. And half-truths, when told to deceive, are lies. Now start from the very beginning! Please."

Tears sprung to Miranda's eyes and a sob caught in her throat. Tearfully she told everything, beginning with the fight with Chris on the playground. She confessed to riding both Starlight and the buckskin mare.

"I meant to tell you, at first. But then when Chris wanted me to come ride Queen, and especially after Starlight got hurt, I was afraid you'd never let me go back. You wouldn't have, would you?"

"Miranda," said Grandpa, sadly shaking his head. "You have so misjudged us. Don't you think we care about you and how you feel?"

"Well, yes, but..."

"What we would have done is to deal with each situation in an honest, open way. We would have gone with you to talk to Mr. Taylor and asked for permission for you to help Chris with Queen. Of course there would have been consequences for riding his horses without permission, maybe enough to keep you from getting on Starlight the second time."

"Oh, I wish I could go back and change that so he wouldn't be lying there all hurt," Miranda moaned. "I'm sorry I lied. The longer I waited to tell the truth, the harder it got. I won't ever lie to you again."

"I certainly hope not," Grandma said. "I'm amazed and disappointed that you lied to so many people."

"I know, Grandma; I'm sorry."

"I told you I'd ground you if you worried me like this again," Grandma said.

"Oh, please don't, Gram. I've learned my lesson. Honest. I just have to help take care of Starlight if Mr. Taylor will let me."

"Well, you did have a good excuse for not calling. But you'll be on probation."

"What do you mean?"

"It means we're giving you another chance," Grandpa explained with a little smile. "If you utter one more lie or forget to let us know where you are at all times, you can't imagine the trouble you'll be in."

Chapter Thirteen

Miranda woke slowly the next morning, closed her eyes and began to go back to sleep.

"Time to get ready for school, sleepy head," said Grandma from the hallway. "If you don't hurry, you'll miss the bus."

Miranda groaned, then sat up quickly and looked at her clock.

"Oh, no! I didn't mean to sleep in. I can't wait to tell Laurie all about yesterday."

But she did miss the bus, and Grandma had to drive her to school. The bell rang loudly as Miranda hurried toward her classroom. She slipped into her seat as Mrs. Penrose began announcing the day's activities. With an eye on the teacher, Miranda wrote on her notebook, "I have so much to tell you," and slid it over to Laurie. As soon as they were dismissed for recess, the girls ran to the swings; their favorite place to sit and talk.

"Laurie, you've got to come back to Shady Hills with me after school!" Miranda exclaimed.

"Why? You know I'm not allowed to go there anymore," Laurie said.

"I know," Miranda said. "But everything is different now. Mr. Taylor knows you didn't let Starlight out. I'm sure it'll be okay now."

"You told him?" Laurie asked in amazement. "When did he get back? What happened?"

Miranda launched into the story with relish, telling every detail of Mr. Taylor's return.

"I was very worried about Chris, but when he came back, I heard all about it. He was so brave, I couldn't believe it. He cantered Queen all the way to town, jumping over two gates. By the time he got to his place he was so scared and stiff that he collapsed when he got off the horse. I guess he fainted because he said they carried him into the store before he came to and told them to call the ambulance. His dad loaded Queen into a horse trailer and told Chris to stay home and go to bed. Chris wouldn't, though. He said he had to see how Mr. Taylor was. He thought I was stuck with a dead man! I thought so too, a couple times. It seemed like forever before the ambulance got there, but it gave me a chance to talk to him."

"Weren't you scared to tell Mr. Taylor?"

"I was a little scared," Miranda admitted. "Well, more than a little. But he didn't look strong enough to do anything, and I had to convince him not to have Starlight put to sleep."

"I hope he'll let us keep coming over there. I'd like to ride Queen some more," Laurie said.

"Oh, I hope so too! When I asked him, he said he'd think about it. You know that when grownups say that, it usually means yes."

"Is he in the hospital?"

"No, when the ambulance people got there, he refused to go with them. They said he needed to get an MRI to see if he had any serious damage. He said he was fine and he wasn't getting off his couch now that he was finally getting warm and comfortable. They kept insisting until he swore at them and threatened to call the sheriff. After they left, I asked if he wanted me to stay. He said he didn't know why I was still there; he'd told me to leave so many times. But he didn't sound mad when he said it. It was more like he was teasing. He even thanked Chris for going after help and then, he asked him when he'd learned to ride!" Miranda laughed. "You should have seen the look on Mr. Bergman's face."

"Oh, no. What did Chris do?"

"He just turned red, and when his dad asked him about it later in the pickup, he said Mr. Taylor was just teasing him."

"You were in their pickup?" Laurie interrupted.

"Yes, Mr. Bergman took me home. I thought that was a pretty good chance for Chris to tell his dad the truth about not really being an expert rider. But even when he was talking to me, telling me all about his ride and everything, he was careful not to let on that he was afraid of horses. Now I know he's more afraid of his dad than he is of Queen."

As soon as Mrs. Bergman stopped the minivan in front of the stables the next morning, Miranda and Laurie ran to the kitchen door and rang the bell. When there was no answer, Miranda opened the door and called, "Mr. Taylor? May we come in?"

"Come in," a feeble voice answered.

Miranda found Mr. Taylor on the sofa where she had left him the night before.

"Are you all right, Mr. Taylor?" she asked, staring at the dark red line in the middle of a big green, blue and yellow bump on the bald part of his head.

"A little weak, and I have a gosh-awful headache," he said. "Would you mind getting me some aspirin from the medicine closet in the bathroom?"

"I'd be happy to," Miranda said. She pointed to Laurie. "Mr. Taylor, this is my friend, Laurie."

"Yes, yes," he said gently. "I remember you. Sorry I accused you of something you didn't do. You remind me..."

Miranda had reached the bathroom and couldn't hear anymore. A terrible odor almost made her gag. Covering her nose, she looked around. Mr. Taylor must have vomited during the night. The toilet was spattered and there was a little on the floor.

"Yuck!" Miranda whispered as she opened the medicine cabinet and found the aspirin.

"Mr. Taylor," she asked as she handed him a glass of water and two aspirin tablets. "Did you get sick last night?"

"Oh, yes. I forgot about the mess. Sorry about that," he apologized. "I just felt too weak to clean it up. I had to crawl back to my couch."

"I'm sorry you felt so bad," Miranda said. "You probably should've gone to the hospital. Shall I call a doctor?"

"No, no doctors!" Mr. Taylor said.

"May we help you to your bed, then?"

"I sleep right here on this sofa. People die in bed, so don't expect to see me there for a long time yet."

"Can we help you clean up and get you something to eat?" offered Laurie.

"I'm all right," he answered. "I know you're aching to get to that horse you call Starlight."

"Let me stay, Mr. Taylor," Laurie begged. "I want to. Miranda can take care of the horse while I tidy up in here."

"Well, you can if you want," he said.

Flashing a smile at Laurie, Miranda said, "I'll see you later, Mr. Taylor."

Starlight was looking out the open top half of the stall door and nickered to her as she rounded the corner of the stables. He limped badly when she led him into the sunshine. After tying him to the paddock fence, Miranda smeared ointment on his wounds and changed his bandages.

"Miranda, will you come help me with Queen as soon as you're through?" Chris called.

As soon as Starlight was back in his clean stall, she hurried to the arena. Chris was just holding Queen's reins and stroking her face.

"What's up?" Miranda asked.

"I rode her," Chris began. "But I was still afraid. I didn't think I would be after last night. I was good

and scared then. All the way to town, I thought I would fall off. I really thought I was going to die!"

"You were very brave, Chris."

"But I'm still a coward."

"You're not! Being scared doesn't mean you're a coward. You proved that last night. I couldn't believe how you cleared that gate!"

"When I saw it coming, I just shut my eyes and held on for dear life!" laughed Chris. "In fact, I rode most of the way with my eyes closed, expecting to be thrown off and trampled at any second."

"But you did it, even though you were scared."

"You told Mr. Taylor you let his colt out, didn't you?" Chris asked, changing the subject.

"Yes," Miranda answered, "I had to."

"No, you didn't have to. I would never have had the guts. I don't have the guts to tell my parents the truth."

"It wasn't as hard as I thought it would be," Miranda offered. "I just got so wound up about Starlight, thinking about him getting killed because of what I did, that it just came out."

"It makes me mad that they are making me ride in the horse show without even asking me what I want. If I ride at all, I want it to be my choice. I'm really scared that when it's not a life and death matter, like it was last night, I will chicken out and embarrass everyone. But I can't tell my parents any of that. I'm scared to say much of anything to them."

"I know it's scary, but if you decide to tell them,

you might feel better," Miranda said. "I sure feel better after telling Mr. Taylor what I did."

"Yeah, but I might not live to feel anything. Well, here comes Mom. I'd better put Queen back in her stall," Chris said, giving the mare an affectionate pat, something Miranda had never seen him do before. "You coming with us?"

"No, I'm going to see if Higgins needs any help before I go. Grandma will come get me."

Miranda walked with Chris as he led Queen to the tack shed to take off her saddle, then went on to find Higgins.

"Oh, Christopher," Miranda heard Mrs. Bergman say. "Let us see you ride before you take the bridle off. We brought your new western saddle. You can try it out."

"Oh, no, Mom. It's late and she's tired."

"I want to see you ride, son," said Mr. Bergman stepping out of the mini-van.

Miranda came back and stood nearby, hoping she could help, somehow.

"But, Dad," Chris began.

"No buts," Mr. Bergman interrupted as he placed the western saddle on Queen's back. "I left the store early to watch you try out your new saddle. Now get on."

Chris's face turned white as he watched his Dad throw the black, silver bedecked western saddle on Queen. The mare shied and threw up her head, not used to the saddle coming at her so suddenly. Mr.

Bergman cursed, straightened the saddle, and cinched it tight. Chris was actually shaking when he struggled to pull himself up to reach the stirrup.

"Hurry up!" Mr. Bergman shouted, as he reached out to help. Queen shied away again, and Chris lost his balance and landed on his side on the ground.

"What's the matter with you?" Mr. Bergman yelled. "Get up and try again. I'll hold her."

Chris's face was red when he stood up.

"I can't do it," he said, staring at the ground.

"What are you talking about?" Mr. Bergman asked angrily. "You won awards for riding at camp. They don't give those out to someone who can't even get on a horse."

"But I didn't win them," Chris mumbled as he tried to blink back his tears.

"What did you say?" asked his mother.

Chris drew circles in the dirt with the toe of his boot and said softly, "I didn't ride at camp."

His father stepped forward, fists clenched.

"What do you mean, you didn't ride?"

Chris swallowed hard and took a deep breath.

"I never wanted to ride when you signed me up, but you never asked me. I've always been afraid of horses. I tried to ride, but I freaked out, so I traded names with another boy and let him ride. He wanted to and I didn't."

Miranda bit her lip as she heard Chris's voice waver and saw tears streaming down his cheeks.

"So that's why the camp counselors looked at me like they thought I was crazy when I called you Christopher. You made us look like fools! Why didn't you tell us?" his father demanded.

"I was afraid to. I knew you'd be disappointed in me."

"So you've kept up a charade all this time? Pretending to ride?" Mrs. Bergman asked in a voice so shrill that Miranda wasn't sure if she was about to scream or cry or both.

"I'm sorry," Chris said, hanging his head.

"Well, it's a sad state of affairs when you're too big a coward to ride, and even worse when you are too afraid of your own parents to tell them the truth!" Mr. Bergman shouted.

Miranda couldn't stand to see Chris cowering before the angry man. He looked so much like a whipped animal.

"I think he's the bravest boy I've ever seen," she interjected.

They all stared at her as if she were an alien or something, so she went on, "He's been practicing every day, even though it scares him. And last night, he rode for help for Mr. Taylor, jumping over two gates and not stopping until he got to town, even though he thought he was going to get killed. He put someone else's life ahead of his own. That's brave; no coward does what he's afraid of."

In the silence that followed, as all three of the Bergmans stared at her, Miranda wished she'd minded her own business.

"You weren't always afraid of horses, Chris." Mrs. Bergman said softly, breaking the silence. "When you were three years old, you loved to ride. Uncle Joe would put you on his big buckskin gelding and lead him around. One time a pheasant flew up under the horse's nose. The horse jumped right out from under you. Then he lunged forward and almost stepped on you. I thought you were going to be trampled right before my eyes." Mrs. Bergman wiped tears from her face and blew her nose. "You didn't want to ride after that, but when you brought home those ribbons, I thought you'd gotten over your fear."

"I still don't understand why you lied to us?" Mr. Bergman shouted.

Chris looked down and mumbled, "I just wanted you to like me."

"Like you?" Mr. Bergman sputtered. "I work my butt off so I can buy nice things for you and your mother, and you think I don't *like* you? I'd say you don't appreciate what it takes to keep this family going! If you did, you'd know how I feel about you. Well, from now on you can do some of the work yourself! You learn to ride that horse or I'll sell it. Then you can work in the store every day after school and all weekend! Which will it be?"

"I'll ride," Chris said, meeting his father's angry gaze for the first time that day. There was a look in his eyes that Miranda had never seen before.

Chapter Fourteen

Chris took the reins and mounted Queen without another word to his parents. They stared as he rode away from them toward the arena.

"Way to go, Chris." Miranda whispered as she turned to go see if she could help Higgins. She found him pushing a wheelbarrow full of dirty shavings to the pile at the end of the lane.

"May I help, Mr. Higgins?" Miranda asked.

"Just one more stall to clean; you may help if you want."

"Your back must be better."

"Yes, much better. The doc said it was a pinched nerve. After one treatment, a hot bath, and some exercises he taught me, I was ready to come home, but John insisted I stay over and keep my Sunday afternoon appointment. I got the first good night's sleep I've had in ages. I wanted to cancel my appointment, but my nephew's stubborn. And after the treatment yesterday, both John and his chiropractor friend told me I shouldn't get back in a car right away. So, I stayed another night and slept like a log! I got back early this morning and ordered myself a new mattress." Higgins smiled at Miranda and added, "Thanks for doing my chores. I knew I could count on you."

"I liked doing it," Miranda replied. "I'm glad you feel better, though."

After they finished cleaning the stall, Miranda hurried back to Starlight. Mr. Taylor was leaning on the bottom half of the door, looking in. Laurie stood beside him. When Miranda joined them, Starlight struggled to his feet, stepped toward them, and nuzzled Miranda's arm.

Mr. Taylor turned to Miranda and said soberly, "You've done a good job, young lady. I didn't think there was any hope for him. It just goes to show what tender loving care can do."

"Thanks," Miranda said hesitantly. "It was all my fault that he got hurt. I'd work the rest of my life to make it up to you."

"No, it's not *all* your fault. My pastures ought to be safe for horses to run in. The wire shouldn't have been there. But you owe me. You got this horse so spoiled he just can't wait for you to come pamper him some more. For that you're going to have to promise to come every day that you can to look after him."

"Oh, Mr. Taylor, thank you. I'll come every single day that Grandma will let me, I promise!"

Miranda couldn't help herself; she hugged Mr. Taylor. For a moment he stood stiffly, taken by surprise, then he relaxed, patted her gently on the back and said, "There, there now, that's quite all right. Just quit getting on my horses without asking me first, will you?"

After much pleading and promising to go to bed early, Laurie was allowed to spend the night with Miranda. The girls had so much to talk about that they hardly took time to eat.

"Finish your supper," Grandma said. "It's almost bedtime. If you end up talking half the night, you won't be sleeping over on a school night again!"

Duly warned, the girls finished eating, cleared the table, and helped with the dishes as they filled Grandma in on the events of the day. They continued to chatter happily as they prepared for bed. Miranda told Laurie about Mr. Bergman's anger at Chris and the look in Chris's eyes.

"I don't know how to explain it. It wasn't fear — something else. Reminded me of a wolf, somehow, you know, how they look in pictures?" Miranda said. "Now, tell me what you did all afternoon in the house with Mr. Taylor."

"Oh, he isn't the mean old grouch I thought he was. I think he just acts that way to cover up his sadness. He told me all about his daughter, Cassy, and said I remind him of her. I put on rubber gloves and tied a towel over my nose when I cleaned up the mess

in the bathroom, and I still almost threw up. But it had to be done. Then I looked at his piano and he told me he bought it for Cassy after seeing her in England. He thought she would come visit him. She loved the piano and played it well, so he bought the best one he could find as a surprise for her."

"But she never came," Miranda said softly, shaking her head.

"No, her mother wouldn't let her. That beautiful piano has been sitting there for nearly thirty years and has never been played!" Laurie exclaimed, "Until today."

"You mean he let you play it?"

"Yes, I told him I love the piano and have been taking lessons since I was five. He didn't say anything for a long time, and then he told me to get some sheet music out of the piano bench. He asked if I could play <u>Fur Elise</u>. I learned it last year. When I played it he cried. He told me he hoped I would come back and play for him again."

"Wow!" Miranda exclaimed. "This is better than Christmas. All kinds of good things are happening at once!"

"Our wishes are coming true," said Laurie. "Let's race to bed."

She darted down the hallway with Miranda on her heels. Giggling, both girls landed on the bed at the same time in a tangle of arms and legs.

Miranda was just dozing off when the telephone aroused her.

"I think she's asleep, can you call back in the morning?" she heard Grandma say. "Well, let me check. If she's awake, I'll let you talk to her."

Miranda got up and met Grandma in the hall. "Who is it?" she asked.

"It's your mother. She has some news for you."

"What is it, Mom?" Miranda asked, anxiously.

"I have some great news, Sweetheart! Sorry to call you so late, but it's an hour earlier here, you know. Sometimes I forget that. Anyway, I just couldn't wait to tell you."

"What is it?" Miranda repeated warily.

"I've found the greatest job. I'm working for a

rich fashion model, taking care of her little boy. The thing is, I get a nice big room of my own and of course the use of the whole house. So no rent to pay."

"That sounds great, Mom. I bet you'll like it."

"Oh, wait. I haven't told you the best part. I just asked the lady if I could have you come live with me, and she said yes! Isn't that wonderful?"

Miranda gulped and sat down.

"Miranda? You're not saying anything. Are you just too happy to speak, or what?"

"It's so sudden, I...I don't know. Is your boy-friend going to live there too?"

"Oh, Randy? No. We broke up. I found out that he already had a girlfriend. Well, she says she's his wife, but he denies it. But he moved back in with her."

"Oh, how awful! Are you sad?"

"I was more mad than sad, I think. But it made me think about what's really important to me. And that's you. I know I haven't been the greatest mom, Miranda, but you'll see, I'm ready to give it another shot. You know I like little kids, and when I found out you could live here with me, I was thrilled. I figured I could get over Randy easy enough with you here. And you can help me with little Kort. You'll adore him. He's just 18 months old, and so cute. I'm sorry it's taken me so long to get my act together, but now we can finally catch up on our lives and be a family again."

"It sounds like you really need me," Miranda squeaked past the lump in her throat. "How soon would I have to go?"

"Why do you ask it like that?" Mom asked. "Don't you want to come? I thought you'd be as happy as I am. Is something wrong?"

"Oh, no, "Miranda answered," not really. It's just, well, I didn't know about it, so I sort of had other plans."

Why did life have to be so complicated, Miranda wondered. She had missed her mom terribly, at first, but now everything she'd wished for seemed to be coming true. Going to California would spoil it all.

"What sort of plans do you have?" Mom asked.

"Well, my best friend and I are helping this horse rancher. He has a horse that got hurt...Well, actually, it got hurt because of me. And the rancher, uh, he got hurt because of me, too."

"Whoa, what do you mean, because of you?"

"It's a long story, Mom. I didn't mean to hurt anybody, but, well, I didn't use very good judgment. Grandma can tell you about it. Anyway, Starlight is my favorite horse in the whole world. He looks for me everyday since I've been taking care of him, and I can tell he's glad to see me!"

"Wow, you do have a lot going on," Mom said. She paused for a moment as Miranda held her breath. "So I take it you'd rather stay there."

"Mom, I don't mean I don't want to be with you. I love you and I'll come if you need me. It's just kind of sad to leave Starlight and my friends behind.

"I see," Mom said. "Does this mean you don't ever want to come?"

"No, Mom, I just mean, well, now is a bad time." Miranda's face burned as she searched for the right words.

"I'm sorry you feel that way. I wanted you to come right away, but maybe it would be better to let me see how this job goes first."

"Oh, are you sure?" Miranda asked, her hopes rising. "When do you think you will know?"

"I don't know, honey. I want us to be together as soon as possible," Mom said. "But I won't upset your plans."

"I don't mean to hurt your feelings, Mom," Miranda sighed, blinking back tears that suddenly stung her eyes. "I'll come whenever you need me. It would just be easier if I knew ahead of time."

Laurie was sitting on a kitchen chair listening, wide eyed, to Miranda's side of the conversation. Miranda shrugged helplessly at her.

"Look, Miranda," Mom said softly. "I love you and want you to be happy. I really miss you, but I'll be okay. It sounds to me like you have some responsibilities there, at least until the rancher and his horse get well. I'll take time to get established in this job, or at least to see how it works out. Okay?"

"Okay, Mom, thanks," Miranda said. "Mom, what about the movie that you auditioned for?"

"Haven't heard anything. I think I would have by now if I'd gotten a part. It's one of those 'don't call us, we'll call you' things."

"I don't suppose you could come for Christmas and see my horse, could you?"

"I doubt it," Mom sighed. "This job is pretty much twenty-four-seven."

"What does that mean?"

"Twenty-four hours a day, seven days a week. That's the only drawback to the job." Mom paused, then said, "I hope it won't always be so hard to leave your horse and your friends."

"I wish I could just bring them, and Grandma and Grandpa to California with me. Or else I wish you could come here."

"Well, I can't see it working that way," Mom said with a laugh. "But, if you're going to wish, you might as well wish big, I guess."

Miranda wiped the tears from her eyes and smiled. "Bye, Mom. Wait, I think Grandma wants to talk to you."

"You okay?" Grandma asked, hugging her before she put the phone to her ear.

Miranda nodded and hugged back.

Snuggled into bed beneath her warm comforter with Laurie by her side, Miranda drew a deep breath, turned over onto her back and stared up into the darkness.

"Miranda?" Laurie asked.

"Hmm?"

"Do you have to go to California soon?"

"No, not right away."

"Do you know when?"

"No."

"I hope it's not for a long time. Unless you want to go," Laurie added. "I don't know what it would be like to have your mother so far away."

"I get really mixed up sometimes, Laurie. I love Mom. But I get mad at her too. Sometimes it seems like she wants me to take care of her. But when she's having a good time with her boyfriends, she doesn't even think about me."

"That must be awful. I miss my dad when he has to go on road trips. He's away from home a lot, selling things. But he always calls and tells us where he is and that he can't wait to get back home."

There was a long pause as Miranda wondered about her own father. What would it be like to get a phone call from him saying that he had been searching for her and was hurrying home to see her?

"Miranda, I hope I didn't make you feel bad."

"You didn't, Laurie. Mom makes me feel bad sometimes, but I have Gram and Grandpa. I always know where they are."

"Was it awful, living with just your mom?"

"No, she's pretty and funny and nice to me." After a pause, Miranda added more honestly, "Well, I was lonely a lot, and I didn't like her boyfriends. But now, well, it might be fun. She'd be at home all the time, and there is a little boy to take care of. She really does love me."

"I didn't mean anything bad about her. It's just a lot different from my family."

"Yeah, I know, Laurie. Don't tell anyone what I said about my mom, will you?"

"Of course not, Miranda! We promised to be best friends. We're going to have a horse ranch together someday. Remember?"

Miranda smiled and reached for Laurie's hand.

"I remember. We'll buy Starlight from Mr. Taylor, and that will be the start of our horse ranch. When your dad gets you a horse, have him get a mare. Then we can breed them and raise the foals. By the time we get through school, we'll already have a start. As soon as the foals are old enough, we'll race them and make money to buy more."

"Yes! We might have to get jobs for a while but we'll buy a big ranch and more mares," Laurie added excitedly.

"Mr. Taylor might let us work for him. We can help Higgins, and when he retires, we can take his place," Miranda said.

"I'm going to name my mare Moonbeam because it matches Starlight," Laurie planned.

"Time to go to sleep, girls," Grandma said from the doorway. "Good night. No more whispering now."

Miranda turned to face Laurie and found her other hand in the dark.

"Good night, Laurie. No matter what the grownups do, we'll always have each other."

"What shall we name our horse ranch?" Laurie whispered, squeezing Miranda's hands.

"Let me think; we'll have Starlight and Moonbeam to start with, so let's think of something about shining lights in a dark sky," suggested Miranda.

But before either of them could come up with a name, they were both sound asleep, their hands still touching.

If you enjoyed *Miranda and Starlight*,
you may also enjoy the rest of the series.

Book 2: *Starlight's Courage,*
Book 3: *Starlight, Star Bright,*
Book 4: *Starlight's Shooting Star,*

And, still to come,

Book 5: *Starlight Shines for Miranda,*
Book 6: *Starlight Comes Home.*

For your convenience, we've provided
an order form on the back of this page
or you may order online:
www.ravenpublishing.net.

Happy Reading and Riding!

Raven Publishing
P.O. Box 2885
Norris, MT 59745
USA

Send check or money order to:
Raven Publishing
P.O. Box 2885
Norris, MT 59745

Or order online: *www.ravenpublishing.net*

For more information, e-mail:
info@ravenpublishing.net
Toll Free: *(866) 685-3545*
Fax: *(406) 685-3599*

$9.00 (U.S.) per book plus $2.00 shipping and handling for first book in a package and $.50 for each additional book.

Name_____

Address_____

City_____State_____Zip_____

Please send me:
_____copies of **Miranda and Starlight**

_____copies of **Starlight's Courage**

_____copies of **Starlight, Star Bright**

_____copies of **Starlight's Shooting Star**

Starlight Shines for Miranda and
Starlight Comes Home will be available in 2004